THE SANTIAGO INHERITANCE

Carol Dougherty

Marjorie,

Thanks for the incredible support you've provided for WRW. It's great to be on this writing path with you.

Dou

Dedication

To the late, great Gary Provost, whose teaching and generosity taught me as much about life as about writing;

To Nushka Provost Stockwell – your love and support have been unwavering through the years, and I am grateful beyond words;

To Brenda Rooney and to Robert, Rebekah, Caitlin, and Andrew – you and Robert taught me that one person can make a difference, and all of you generously made me feel as if I were part of your family;

To Lorin Oberweger and WRW students and staff – past, present, and future – your companionship on the path has been one of the great gifts of my life;

and to my parents, Pat and Doc; my sister and brother, Karen and Kevin; and their families, Tom, Hope, TJ, Krista, Michael, Brendan, Robin, Faith, Peyton, Evan, Hadley, Harper, Anna, Hattie, Lane, and Quinn – thank you for your presence on this journey.

Note

This book was written a number of years ago, and occurs at a specific time in history – toward the end of the Pinochet regime in Chile.

At that time personal computers were rare, most operated in a Basic universe, and the security options were primitive and simplistic compared to what is available now.

Table of Contents

Chapter One

Santiago, Chile

July 10, 1988

Could you know someone so well that he became a stranger? Or had he always been a stranger that you convinced yourself you knew?

Anna watched Romo over the top of an open book. Her husband hunched above the mahogany desk, rivers of sweat streaking his white shirt. He scrawled notes in the margins of his manuscript, and muttered under his breath. The scratch of his pencil and the hiss of the coffee pot on the bookcase were the only other sounds in the study.

Anna turned the page without reading a word. Romo massaged his scalp, leaving tufts of thick, black hair sticking out at erratic angles. It was a familiar sight to Anna, and in the early years of their marriage she'd found it endearing. After fifteen years, it had become an infuriating reminder that he was absorbed in his work, and not in her.

"Aren't you hot?" she asked.

"What?" Romo didn't look up.

"I said, aren't you hot? That sun is beating down on your back." She got up. "Do you want me to close the blinds?" She stood close behind him and ran her fingernails down his spine.

"I don't care," he said. His focus never wavered from the manuscript in front of him. Anna dropped her hand and glowered at his back.

She wandered over to the bookcase under the window and drew out a copy of *Grimm's Fairy Tales*. Her fingers caressed the faded green cover, its leather soft from constant handling. Perched on the corner of her desk, she leafed through it. "Snow White and Rose Red," "The Goose Girl," "The Bremen Town Musicians." Most of her childhood friends had lived between the covers of a book.

Anna closed the book and looked around the room. The study was too small to hold more than two desks, two chairs, and the bookcase that sat under the window. Many of her books were still in boxes, because the shelves didn't have room for all of her old friends. And Romo refused to spend her money on a bigger house, even though she could well afford it.

It was her money. Inherited when her parents died, and sitting in a bank thanks to Romo's stubbornness. He didn't mind spending what she earned; only what she inherited. His salary and her royalties paid for the house and the once-a-week maid.

She glanced back at Romo. He was still involved in his work. She put the fairy tales back on the shelf and noticed a bright green water pistol lying next to the coffee pot. Their younger son had been tormenting his brother the night before, and Romo had confiscated Pablo's weapon. Maybe that would cool him off. Or heat him up. Stifling a giggle, she picked up the water pistol and took aim.

A stream of water caught him between the shoulder blades. He jumped up, and she doubled over in laughter.

"What the hell's the matter with you?" he said. Romo pulled the damp shirt away from his skin and glared at her.

"Can't you take a joke?" she said with a grin.

Romo responded with a cold stare. "Grow up," he said. He sat down and turned his back to her. Anna felt the hot flush of humiliation sweeping through her body.

"Damn you!" she said. Her voice broke on the words. Romo glanced up. Anna hurled the water pistol at his face. He ducked. It struck the corkboard on the wall next to their desks and a shower of papers cascaded to the floor.

"What are you doing?" he cried. Romo leaned over to shove the mess under his desk. He straightened up and waited for an explanation, but Anna couldn't trust her voice enough to speak. Romo shook his head and bent over his manuscript.

She fought to calm herself. At the first hint of

tears, Romo would walk out. Long gone were the days when he'd try to comfort her. She took a deep breath and said, "You work too much."

"What are you talking about?" asked Romo. His attention was still on the papers in front of him.

"You ignored me at breakfast," said Anna. She braced herself against the desk with sweaty palms. "You've ignored me all morning. I don't like being ignored."

Romo slid the papers inside a folder, swiveled the chair to face her and settled back. "All right," he said. He tapped his pen in a light rhythm on the folder. "You have my complete attention. What do you want?"

"You," said Anna. She stopped, afraid her voice would betray her.

"What do you mean?"

"I mean I want you to pay some attention to your family."

Romo's black brows lifted, his face darkened with anger. "What are you talking about?" he said.

"Your sons, Luis and Pablo. You remember them, don't you? And me, your wife, the woman you married?"

Anna folded her arms tight against her body, battling the temptation to reach out to him. It would be so easy to end this argument the way they had ended so many others. The only tenderness left between them was in bed, and she needed tenderness. As if he had read her mind, Romo held out a hand to her.

"Anna," he began.

She closed her eyes, determined not to give in this time. "We're right in front of you," she said. "But you're so busy with your writing and with your politics you never even notice us."

"Don't be ridiculous."

"Ridiculous-" Anna turned to the window so he couldn't see the pain and longing on her face. It was useless. Once upon a time he would have dropped everything to make her happy. She heard him sigh behind her.

"I'm sorry you feel neglected," he said. She heard his chair creak and papers rustle. He was back at work. A sucker punch would have been kinder. She spun around.

"Apology not accepted!" she snapped. He ignored her words. "I want to know what's going on," she said. "You've been completely buried in your work - even more than usual. What's so important you can't find time for your family?" She reached over his shoulder and snatched at his manuscript. His hand caught hers in mid-air.

"Anna that's enough," said Romo. His voice was low and controlled. Anna tried to pull her hand free. He instantly released it. He got to his feet and looked down on her with a perplexed expression.

"No," she said, "It isn't enough." Her neck ached from the strain, but she refused to look away first. "I want some answers. You can't keep pretending nothing is wrong."

"What's wrong isn't with me-"

"-No, of course not," she interrupted. "It never is. Everything is my fault."

"I never said that."

He was so blind. Why couldn't she hate him

when he was like this? Why did she still want him? She forced her mind back to the subject.

"It is politics," she said. "Isn't it?"

"Never mind." Romo walked over to the window and stared out.

"Damn it, don't walk away from me when I'm talking to you!" she said. "Just because I don't get upset like you do over every stupid person who gets himself arrested, you act like I don't know what's going on."

"Leave it, Anna."

"You aren't the only one who reads the papers and watches the news." She waited in impotent fury for a response. "Damn it, talk to me!"

"I can't," he said, clenching his fists. The muscles in his neck were taut as ropes. "You don't listen."

"I'm listening now," Anna insisted. She tried to steady her breathing.

"No, you're not." He pivoted and studied her. "You refuse to see what goes on around you. You've lived in Chile for almost twenty years, you've lived with me for fifteen years, yet you can pretend that everything is fine."

"The coup was fifteen years ago, Romo." His polite attention mocked her. She struggled for the words that would convince him, and bridge the gap. "I'm the daughter of a diplomat. I know what I'm talking about."

"You're an American," he said. "You never lived *there* for more than a few years at a time. You-"

"I've seen a lot more of the world than you have," she shot back.

"Living in embassies, growing up as a member of the privileged elite doesn't qualify you as an expert on politics," he said. "I suppose you see Pinochet as a humanitarian, not a bloody dictator?"

She threw up one hand, like a traffic warden. "Don't start with that line about disappearances and torture, please," she said. "You know those are just stories." She leaned against the desk, as if needing its support for her next words. "You are right about one thing, though."

"What's that?"

"Everything is not fine with us."

There was silence for a moment. Something flashed across Romo's face. His lips tightened into a grimace and he closed his eyes. For a second she thought it was pain. Then his face was composed again and she dismissed the thought as absurd. He broke the silence with an effort.

"I want a divorce."

There was a roaring sound in her ears. Romo's words pounded against her brain - "Divorce - I want a divorce." The pounding was unbearable.

"I'll get it," said Romo. He was out of the study and running down the stairs before Anna realized the pounding she heard was at the front door, not in her head. She charged after him.

Romo opened the door. Two men in suits and trench coats shouldered their way into the front hall. One man was dark and stocky, the other blond and slight. They can't come in, thought Anna, still reeling from the bomb he'd dropped. I don't care who they are; Romo and I have to talk.

"Are you Romulo Peregrino?" asked the dark,

stocky man.

"Who wants to know?" said Romo. Their grim appearance caused the first stirring of alarm in Anna. Romo's massive form moved to block her view. She winced at his aggressive tone and threatening attitude. Romo never gave ground. To anyone.

He was shutting her out of this, too. She slid from behind Romo to get a better look at them.

The man ignored Anna. "Police. Are you Rom-"

Anna interrupted. "Of course he is. What do you want?" Romo was no criminal. This was ridiculous.

They continued to ignore Anna. The dark one motioned to Romo. "Come with us."

"Why?" Romo asked, "What do you want?" He silenced Anna's protest with a glance.

"You're under arrest," the man said. "Let's go." Neither stranger moved, but Anna saw their bodies tense up. Why were they arresting Romo? And why did he have to antagonize them?

"No," said Romo. He crossed his arms and watched them.

"Wait! What do you think you're doing?" Anna said. "You can't just burst in here-"

"Anna, stay out of it," said Romo. He turned to emphasize his warning with a frown.

The slight, blond intruder leaped. He seized Romo and jerked his arms behind him. Anna gasped. Romo struggled in vain. She stepped forward to protest. The dark man barred her progress. Peering around him, Anna was shocked to see that the wiry strength of the blond man held Romo's huge frame with ease.

"What do you want?" Romo snarled. He strained to break free and Anna's muscles tensed in sympathy with his efforts.

"You," said the dark man. He frisked Romo up and down, his hands slapping Romo's legs, arms and torso. Anna flinched with every slap.

Romo's face was scarlet. The blond man's grip tightened. Romo thrust an elbow back into his stomach. With a grunt, the man gave Romo's right arm a vicious twist. Romo tried to stomp on the blond man's instep. The dark man grabbed Romo's shirt, pinning Romo between the two of them. Romo aimed a head butt at the dark man, but the man gave him a quick uppercut to the jaw. Romo sagged to his knees. The blond man whipped out a pair of handcuffs and snapped them on Romo's wrists. Anna stood, paralyzed.

The dark man grinned and cocked his fist for another blow. "Stop it!" cried Anna. Astounded to find she could move again, she ran forward and clutched the dark man's arm. He knocked her to the floor with a powerful backhand. She collided with the wall. Her knee banged painfully against the tile and she cried out.

Romo struggled to his feet. The blond man grabbed a fist full of his hair and yanked. "You make one more move, and you can watch while we kill her." Anna looked up, her heart racing. Romo became suddenly still. The blond man pushed him toward the door. "Let's go."

"Wait!" said Anna. Ignoring the throbbing in her knee, she found the strength to get up off the floor. "Wait, where are you taking him?"

"Shut up," growled the dark, stocky man.

Turning to his partner, he said, "Get going." The blond man shoved Romo outside and hustled him into the sedan parked at the curb.

Anna lunged for the door. The dark man blocked her way. Steely fingers curled around her upper arm and brought her to an abrupt halt. Where were the neighbors? Didn't anyone see what was going on?

The car door slammed shut. The man looked Anna up and down, as if seeing her for the first time. "Too bad," he said. "We could have had fun with you." He glanced out at the waiting car, then back at Anna. "Keep your mouth shut," he said. "Don't talk to anyone." Before she could reply he released her, strode across the lawn, slid behind the wheel and drove away.

Anna watched the tail lights disappear around the corner. She looked at the houses on either side and across the street. The neighborhood was deserted, a ghost town. It didn't make sense. At this time of day there should be someone around. She shook her head in a futile attempt to clear it, then went inside and closed the front door behind her. The living room clock chimed the quarter hour. Only ten minutes ago she and Romo had been fighting. He had asked for a divorce. Now, he was gone. And she didn't know where or why.

She sank down on the hall steps. What had just happened? She tried to think it through, but her mind seemed to travel its own path. Romo was gone, but it wasn't the way she'd imagined it. More than once, she'd fantasized about kicking him out. But she hadn't meant it. And he'd suggested divorce. He couldn't have meant it either. But arrested? That possibility had never occurred to her. She sat on the bottom step, the tiled floor of the entryway cool on her bare feet, and tried to break through the fog.

She hadn't done the breakfast dishes. She couldn't leave them sitting in the sink. Romo hated dirty dishes in the sink. Anna jumped up.

In the kitchen, she threw open the faucets. Water gushed out. The lemon scent of the dish detergent filled the room while suds filled the sink. There was a sharp pain in her abdomen; panic was gnawing a hole in her stomach. She had to remember everything that had happened that morning. There had to be a clue to explain Romo's arrest somewhere.

The boys had been up and dressed as usual, breakfast punctuated with the normal squabbles. Romo had glanced through the morning paper, teased the boys, and ignored her. She'd even stolen his favorite sweatshirt that morning and worn it to try and get a rise out of him. He hadn't noticed.

Anna slammed the faucets shut. She dropped a stack of plates into the sink. Suds flew up and dotted her forehead. An impatient swipe of her forearm wiped them off. She snatched up a handful of silverware and flung it into the suds. Spoons clattered against bowls. Her dishcloth plunged in and out of soapy glasses.

The boys had gotten off to school on time. After they left, she and Romo fought over whose turn it was to make the coffee upstairs in the office.

Anna dropped a glass in the sink and grabbed a towel to dry her hands. The coffeepot had been going strong when the men interrupted them. She raced upstairs. The acrid odor of burnt coffee met her at the study door. She turned off the pot and poured a cup. She gulped the bitter brew, scalding her mouth.

On Romo's desk, his manuscript was still neatly inside its folder. Anna flipped through it, searching for clues. His corrections and changes covered the pages in bold, red slashes.

Who could she call? Romo had been estranged from his family for years, and they lived further south, in Valdivia. Since her own parents had died, she had no close family except for a great aunt Florence in Buffalo, New York, whom she'd never met. Emilio, and Tomas and Maria were their only real friends, but the man had said not to call anyone. It might be wise to listen.

She slumped into Romo's oversized chair and read the article. She finished, and then read it through again. It was the usual boring political analysis. Nothing that would explain his arrest.

She put her mug on top of the pages and sighed. She had been watching him that morning, instead of writing. Until the fight. *I want a divorce.* His words echoed in her mind. It was impossible to reconcile that statement with the Romo she first knew.

"I don't believe in divorce, Anna." Romo pushed his books aside and leaned across the table in the university cafeteria.

Anna was puzzled by his sudden gravity. She'd only known him a few weeks, and his moods could be disconcerting. His fingers teased the palm of her hand, and a wave of excitement swept away all memory of their discussion. The lightness of his touch always surprised her. He reminded her of the bear in Snow White and Rose Red, a gentle giant. She sometimes fantasized that her love had turned him into a prince.

"You're daydreaming again," said Romo, with a chuckle.

"No, I'm not," she said, and pulled her hand away. Anna could feel the blush creeping up her neck. She returned to the earlier subject, hoping he'd forget to notice her reddening face. "I didn't realize you were such a staunch Catholic."

Romo nodded. He opened his mouth to speak, then closed it. He frowned at the table.

"I'm sorry," said Anna, "Did I offend you?"

"No, of course not." Romo looked up and smiled. "I just don't talk about it very often."

"Why not?"

"It's a long story."

"I have plenty of time." This time it was Anna who reached across the table to take his hand. She glanced around the student cafeteria. The place was almost deserted except for a few other people over by the stairs. "No one else will hear," she said.

"My parents wanted me to leave school when I turned sixteen," said Romo. His voice was low, and he looked down at their clasped hands while he spoke. "I was always in trouble, anyway, and they couldn't understand why I wanted to stay."

"Why were you always in trouble?"

"I fought with the teachers."

"Why?" said Anna.

Romo thought for a moment. "The first time I got in trouble I was only eight. My best friend didn't have a clean uniform because his mother was sick, but the teacher was going to punish him anyway. I wouldn't let him."

"What did you do?"

"I threw a wastebasket at the teacher," he said, with a grin. "They sent me home with a note to my parents." His grin faded. "That was the first time my father beat me."

Anna's grip tightened on his hand. He laid his other hand on top of hers, as if to reassure her he was fine.

"Anyway, when I refused to leave school, my father threw me out. He said if I wouldn't help support the other kids I could at least take care of myself."

"Where did you go?" said Anna. She tried to keep the tremor out of her voice, but she knew he had heard it when he lifted her hand to his lips and kissed it.

"Padre Dominic let me live in the basement of the church," Romo explained. His voice was stronger. "I was the janitor for the church, and he gave me a place to sleep and let me share his meals."

"What did your father say?"

"I don't know." Romo rubbed his eyes. "I stayed at the church for two years before I went away to university. I saw my mother and my brothers and sisters every week." Anna felt her heart constrict at the grief in his voice. "My father forbade them to speak to me. They obeyed, afraid my father would find out and beat them." Anna laid her cheek against his hand. She didn't know what to say. Her own parents had been so loving. So indulgent and understanding.

"Padre Dominic was my family until he died last year," said Romo. "I saw the church through different eyes because of his love." His hand caressed her cheek. He lifted her chin and his eyes met hers with a passionate intensity. "But we'll never need to *worry about divorce."*

I want a divorce. What could have brought the man she loved, a devout Catholic, to the point of asking for a divorce? How could she not see it coming? "I can't think about it now," she cried. The sound of her voice startled her. She had to stop thinking about Romo and divorce. She needed to figure out why he'd been arrested.

It had been a long time since he had confided in her. He'd become secretive about his writing and what he did when he was out of the house. There had to be a political connection to the arrest. It was the strain of politics that was tearing their marriage apart.

Damn it, Romo, she thought. What did you do to make them arrest you? What do I say to Pablo and Luis, who worship you? Sorry guys. They arrested your father, but I don't know why and I don't know where he is or when he'll be back. She shivered. It sounded too much like one of Romo's disappearance stories.

The doorbell rang and shattered her trance. Maybe it had been a mistake. Maybe they brought him back. Anna raced downstairs and flung open the door. It wasn't Romo.

Chapter Two

On the other side of the door was a distinguished silver-haired gentleman in a tailored suit. He didn't look a day over fifty-five, though Anna knew he was at least sixty. In spite of his moderate height, her head barely reached above his shoulders. His handsome, tanned face wore a serious expression.

"Emilio, hello," managed Anna. She swallowed her disappointment and tried to smile.

He stepped inside with a pantherlike grace, and closed the door behind him. "How are you, Anna?"

"I'm so glad you're here." She'd known Emilio since she was a baby. He would help her. Anna embraced him; his cheek was as cool and smooth as that of her younger son. It was a familiar and welcome touch, as familiar as the powerful sandalwood scent of his cologne. Suddenly she felt safe and protected in his arms.

Her father had been posted to Chile right before she was born. Emilio moved in diplomatic circles in those days, and the two families had become close friends. Even after they moved on to other countries, Anna and her parents returned to Chile for two weeks every winter to ski with Emilio and his wife. When she and Romo got married, Emilio gave Romo a job with his magazine. Now that her parents and Emilio's wife were dead, he was her only link to the past. Her only family outside of Romo and the boys.

"I'm so glad you're here," she repeated. "I need your help. Romo-"

"I understand Romo has been detained," Emilio said. He took Anna's arm and drew her into the living room.

"You know?" Her heart skipped a beat. He had come to help her.

He nodded, but didn't meet her eyes. "Yes, I heard about it a few minutes ago and came right over." He gestured to Anna to sit on the love seat and sat down beside her. "Why don't you tell me what happened."

She shuddered and took a deep breath. "It was right after breakfast. We were upstairs - working." She stopped, remembering the fight. Emilio didn't need to hear about that. "These two men showed up at the door," she said. "They rang the bell and took Romo away. They didn't say why or where or when I can see him. Will you help me, Emilio? You know people, you could-"

"What was he working on?" he broke in. Anna looked at him, puzzled. He appeared to be studying the onyx ring on his right hand, and didn't look up.

"An article, I think." She hesitated, "For your next issue probably."

"Nothing else?" he asked. She frowned and shook her head. What was he getting at? Why wouldn't he look at her?

Emilio got up and crossed over to the mantel. He picked up a brass elephant she'd given her parents one Christmas in India, and examined it as he spoke. "Romo's articles were becoming - a problem."

"A problem?" Anna repeated.

"Yes," he replied, "The material was inflammatory. He had no discretion."

"But you're his publisher," she said. "You edit his articles. How could he get anything printed if you didn't approve? I don't understand."

"There are a lot of things you don't understand."

Anna struggled to follow his words. Her mind felt foggy, but she tried to pay attention.

"Romo took many risks. I warned him several times that he was treading on dangerous ground, but he ignored me."

"He never mentioned anything to me," said Anna. "Anyway, none of that matters now. You'll help us, won't you?"

Emilio was silent, his face impassive, turning the elephant over and over in his well-manicured hands. She watched him, fascinated and uneasy. She had never seen him like this. The man she knew would

18

do anything for her or for her family.

"Emilio, you were my parents' friend! You've been a part of my family since I can remember..." Her voice trailed off. He remained silent. "You've been one of my closest friends since my parents died. Why don't you want to help me?"

"Of course I'll help you," he said. He returned the elephant to its precise spot on the mantel and faced her. "I know exactly how to help you, my dear."

"Oh, thank you, Emilio." Anna's voice was as warm as her smile. Her smile faded when he sat beside her and took her hand. She could feel the tension in his fingers, and it frightened her.

"You want Romo to be safe." His right hand held both of hers while the left one lay on top. His hands were cool and smooth, just like his cheek. His touch no longer seemed so familiar or welcome.

"Yes, of course." Anna tried to edge away from him, but his grip tightened on her hands.

"Well I can help you, but you must do exactly as I tell you." He held up a hand when she tried to speak. "Wait. You will go out with me - dinner, concerts, the theatre."

"But how will-"

"-How will that help?" Emilio said. She nodded. "As long as you show that we are close, and that we are very good friends, Romo will be fine."

"But why?" she asked. "Why would the people who put Romo in prison care about you - or me?"

He didn't answer. His hand moved up to touch her face, then her hair. He unclipped the barrette that held her ponytail and released the luxuriant tresses.

"I've always liked your hair," he murmured. He twisted one curl in his fingers. "Like midnight. But the face that it frames is white and pure, not dark like the mestizo. You always were a beautiful child."

"Emilio!" Anna tried to pull away. His iron grip held her.

"Don't move," he said. He brushed one curl against his lips. Her heart pounded. She could feel the blood rush to her face. The heavy, sweet smell of his cologne made her sick. She let out a sigh of relief when he stood up. He forced up her chin with the tips of his fingers.

"You have a choice, Anna." His voice was soft, barely more than a whisper. She strained to hear his words. "You can cooperate with me, or Romo will die."

Anna jumped to her feet. "Did *you* have him put in prison?" she said.

"Don't ask questions and you won't get hurt!" Emilio said. "Now sit down and listen!"

She sat back down on the edge of the sofa, her legs trembling too much to hold her weight.

"Your husband was very stupid," he said. "I tried to warn him, but he chose not to pay attention."

"Romo never told me-"

"Shut up! I don't have all day to waste here." The civilized veneer had cracked, and Anna had a glimpse of an Emilio who was a stranger to her.

She waited, rigid and speechless.

"When I heard about this week's article I knew we had to act. Since he wouldn't cooperate, we'll have to convince him."

"But you-" she began.

He cut her off, "Yes, I'm his publisher. That's beside the point."

Anna sought for some sign of reassurance in Emilio's face. There was none.

"You can help Romo or you can kill him."

"How?"

"You will do what I tell you. You will not tell anyone anything. Do you understand?" He towered menacingly over the love seat.

"Yes."

"Good," he said. "Your story is this: Romo is on an assignment. It is confidential, you have no idea when he'll be back, and you don't expect to hear from him in the meantime."

Anna nodded.

"You will not discuss this with your children or your friends. If you do - " She held her breath as the pause lengthened. "If you do," he said, bending over and thrusting his face close to hers, "Your husband will die, slowly and painfully. Your sons will be taken from you and sent away. And you will wish you were dead."

He straightened and paced the length of the living room. The precision of his words and movements hypnotized her.

"Your life will go on as always. See your friends, do your work, go to church. Make sure everything appears normal."

He stopped in front of her. "You will see me whenever I choose, and you will make everyone believe that we are very - good - friends." Anna felt her face flush at the emphasis on the last three words.

Emilio glanced at his watch.

"In fact we *will* be very good friends. In every way. If I give you a present, you accept it. You will be grateful, you will be charming, and you will be loving."

"Emilio, no-" she choked.

He temporarily abandoned his harsh demeanor. "Anna, cooperate," he said gently. Her head and shoulders sagged. "Think about it. If you were anyone else, if I were *not* your friend, this would be much worse." He touched her shoulder. She shuddered and he pulled back. "Usually they send at least five soldiers."

Anna stared at the floor. Her mind flashed back to Romo's captor looking her over and saying it was too bad. Her hands gripped the edge of the love seat. If only this were a nightmare so she could wake up. Emilio lifted her to her feet, but she bowed her head.

"You are lucky, Anna," he said. The harsh tone was back in his voice. "If it weren't for me you would have been severely beaten by now. You'd have been raped by the soldiers. You'd have been lucky to survive. If you had survived, imagine what would have happened when your sons came home from school."

She raised her head. "My sons?"

Emilio nodded, "Your sons. They would have been lucky to be shot. More likely the soldiers would have tortured them for the pleasure of hearing the screams."

Her sons. Pablo and Luis. She couldn't let them be hurt. She spoke softly. "I'll do whatever you want."

22

"Good." He stroked her hair and she forced herself to remain motionless. Her stomach heaved and she swallowed hard.

"When will you be back?" she asked.

"Tomorrow night. I will pick you up at seven for dinner." He leaned over and kissed her forehead. His cool lips burned against her skin. "And don't get any brilliant ideas about running away, or sending them out of the country." His voice was as gentle as if he were telling her he loved her. "I'll be watching them. One move to leave and they're gone. Goodbye my dear." She made herself smile until he walked out the door. The smile disappeared and she dropped back down on the love seat.

His friend. His very good friend. She buried her face in her hands. Tears trickled through her fingers and dampened her jeans. Anna bit her lip to keep the screams inside. She tasted blood, but she couldn't allow herself the luxury of a scream.

Rage, frustration and panic swept her in turn. She thought of her innocent young sons and wiped her tears on the sleeve of Romo's sweatshirt. She would do anything to protect Pablo and Luis.

Anna licked the blood from her bottom lip. Emilio had left her with no alternatives. She was shut tight in a box with no way out, suffocating.

It was Romo's fault. None of this would have happened if he'd listened to her and stayed out of politics. Rage engulfed her. What had he written that could have wreaked such havoc on their lives?

What *had* he written? She could at least find that out. She raced upstairs. In the study, Romo's writing was neatly organized in a gunmetal gray, two-drawer file cabinet that supported half of her desk. The top drawer stuck for a moment, then flew open when she yanked with both hands.

After twenty minutes of flipping through every file in the cabinet Anna sat back on her heels. Emilio was crazy. Romo's articles were all about other countries. He never wrote about Chile. She read through the story in her hands again. It was a commentary on apartheid in South Africa. It had nothing to do with Chile.

She replaced the clipping in its folder. It didn't matter what she found. It wouldn't change what Emilio had said. She was going to have to cooperate with him if she wanted to keep her sons safe. And Romo alive. She couldn't breathe.

Anna closed the drawer and leaned back against its cold, hard surface. She wrapped her arms around her knees and hugged them close to her chest. What would Romo think of the ultimatum she'd been given? Men had such a strange sense of honor. Romo thought nothing of using passionate lovemaking to manipulate her into doing what he wanted. Yet he had been furious shortly after Luis was born, when she accepted a small loan from Tomas so she could buy some groceries. He had pawned his wedding ring so he could immediately repay Tomas, and hadn't spoken to her for two days. She had been astounded to learn that her husband would have gone hungry rather than ask for help. Would he rather she let him die and their sons be tortured than suffer the shame of knowing his wife slept with another man to save him?

Did Emilio seriously expect her to make love to him? Her stomach churned at the thought. How could she go to bed with a man who had been like a second father to her? How could he even ask it?

24

She had never felt so alone. Not even when her parents died. She'd had Romo then. And Emilio. She shuddered. There was no one to help her protect her sons. If only her parents were still alive. Her father, strong and laughing. A busy career diplomat, who had time to be a hero for his little girl. She had adored her mother only a little less than her father. If they were alive they'd find a way to help her.

She considered Romo's best friend, Tomas. It was too risky. Emilio had been their close friend for even more years, and look what he was doing. How could she have lived in Chile all these years and only have two friends? She knew the diplomatic service did that. You never stayed anywhere too long, and you had to be careful whom you knew. Like Kat.

Anna leaned her head back against the file cabinet and closed her eyes. More than twenty-five years later the memory of Kat still hurt. She was eight. Her father was posted to India at the time. Her parents had been delighted she'd finally found a friend. Delighted, until they discovered Kat was Katerina, daughter of the East German military attaché. Daddy had explained that for security reasons they couldn't be friends, and bought her a turtledove as an apology. Anna had never allowed herself to get close to anyone after that. Not until Romo. And Emilio had threatened to kill Romo if she talked. She believed him.

Wasn't there anyone she could trust? A picture of Padre Vincent flashed into her mind. He was their pastor at the church of San Joaquin, and a kindly old priest. Anna didn't know him well, but if she spoke to him in the confessional, in secret, surely he could help. At least she could talk about it. He wouldn't know who she was. He couldn't break the seal of the confessional. She glanced at her watch. It was just half past eleven. Confessions were from eleven to noon every day before the noon mass.

Panic paralyzed her. Should she trust anyone, even a priest? What if Padre Vincent were working with the government? What if Emilio snatched her boys from school anyway, to ensure her compliance?

Smothering her rising panic, Anna jumped up and hurried downstairs to the kitchen. She grabbed her keys from a hook on the wall and said a silent prayer as she went out the kitchen door.

Chapter Three

Anna entered the stone church. She stopped inside the door to give her eyes a chance to adjust to the dim light. A handful of people were scattered through the wooden pews, most of them kneeling in prayer.

Dipping her fingers into the white marble holy water font, she genuflected, made the sign of the cross, and entered the closest pew. The peaceful hush of the cool church wrapped itself around her. The wood of the kneeler was painful against her bruised knee.

From the time she was a young child, Anna had loved going to church. When no grownups were around, she would light votive candles with the long matches she found nearby, and say a prayer with each one. Years later, someone told her she was supposed to pay for the candles. She never bothered with them after that.

The wooden door of the confessional in the left sacristy creaked when an elderly man came out. He shuffled to a pew in the middle of the church, pulled out a rosary and began to mumble his prayers. A young boy of about fifteen went into the empty confessional. There were no other penitents waiting.

Anna had always wondered what other people told the priest while they were in there. She had been taught well by the sisters, and never entered the confessional without preparing a list of her sins. It was a sin to waste the priest's time.

The faint drone of the old man's prayers was punctuated by the click, click, click of his rosary beads. Anna debated again the wisdom of coming to church. What could a priest do? She didn't know, but coming to the church for sanctuary was as instinctive to her as the urge to pick up a book when she was unhappy. The creaking door announced the successful absolution of another sinner, and Anna got up before anyone else could go in.

She closed the flimsy door behind her and knelt. A voice prompted her from the other side of the grate, "Yes?" She recognized Padre Vincent's kind voice. She visualized his snow-white mane and gentle smile, and was comforted.

"Yes, my child?"

"Oh. Bless me Padre, for I have sinned," she said. "Oh - no - I'm sorry, I haven't sinned. I mean, I *have* sinned, but that's not why I'm here."

"Why are you here?" he asked.

"Padre, it's my husband." Anna stopped. Misgivings paralyzed her. Should she trust him? He might be a priest, but he was a man, and was it safe to talk to him?

"What is wrong with your husband?" His even, unemotional tone allayed her fears.

"Well, it's not exactly my husband," she said. "It's the police. At least I *think* it's the police."

"Is your husband in trouble with the police?" he asked. She could hear his vestments rustling.

"They came this morning-"

"It sounds like you should be talking to a lawyer, not a priest." His voice rose half an octave.

"But they said-"

"-My child, I really cannot help in these state matters." His agitation annoyed her. State matters? What was wrong with him? She was in trouble and needed help. A priest was supposed to help people in trouble.

The rustling of his vestments became more pronounced. "I am here to absolve sinners," he said firmly.

"But Padre, can't you even listen to me? I need to talk to someone." She marveled at herself, pleading for this coward's understanding. She sounded like a stranger. Anna Kelly never begged for anything.

"You must pray and trust in the Lord." His voice was assured again now that he was back on familiar ground.

"How can you tell me to trust in God when my

husband-"

"I'm afraid that's all I can suggest." He cut off any compromising words. "Try saying a rosary each night. That will comfort you."

"Thank you Padre." She stood abruptly in the dark, hot little box. "You've been a great help."

She banged the door of the confessional against the wall when she left. The old man frowned at her from his pew. The quiet calm of the church was stifling, and Anna hurried out through the side door.

The kitchen door burst open. Anna almost dropped the mug of hot tea that was halfway to her mouth. She cast a startled glance at the clock. Several hours had passed since she got back from church. She'd been sitting here, drinking one cup of tea after another, thinking. Pablo's tempestuous entrance brought her back to reality. With unsteady hands, Anna set the mug on the table and smiled.

Eight-year-old Pablo was the image of his father. He was nearly as tall as his older brother, but where Luis was like a lithe and slender gazelle, Pablo was more of a husky, young bull. His sturdy frame and curly black hair made him look like Romo in miniature. He rushed at her, arms wide.

"Mama!" he crowed, "My team won!"

Anna braced herself and caught him close. They won't touch him, she vowed, not if I have to lie down for the whole Chilean army.

He stepped back and triumphantly waved a tattered blue ribbon. "Look, we even got prizes."

"It's beautiful," she said. She noticed a telltale

triangle of white paper peeking out of his pants pocket. "But you got something else today, didn't you?"

"Everyone on our team got a ribbon that says First Place," he said. He laid the ribbon in front of her, a stubby finger pointing out the gold lettering. "And the other team didn't get anything."

"That's wonderful," she agreed. Anna's heart twisted at his attempts to distract her. Pablo's resemblance to his father didn't end with his looks. "Now what about your report card?"

Pablo drew a grubby white paper out of his pants pocket and handed it over. He regarded his mother gravely while she examined his second grade report card.

"Can I have some cookies?" he asked. "Are you taking me to practice? Where's Papa?" Anna poured him a glass of milk.

"Your father had to go out of town unexpectedly. I'm not sure when he'll be back." She hoped he'd be coming back. She opened the cookie jar and offered it to him.

"Won't he be here for my game this week?" Grinning, Pablo took several cookies.

"I don't know." She'd never lied to her children before. Was this to be the first of many lies? She looked at the report card again. "Your teacher seems to think all you want to do is play soccer."

"I *like* soccer," he insisted.

"I know. But you have to learn math and spelling, too, or no more soccer."

"Mama!"

"I'll get Luis to help you with your homework."

31

She glanced at the clock. Luis should have been home by now. Where was he? "Where is your brother?"

"I don't know." He grabbed another cookie and dunked it in his milk.

"Didn't you see him today?" Anna twisted the report card in her hands, waiting for Pablo's reply.

"Nope."

"Why not?" she prodded. Emilio had left before noon. Luis was still in school then. But would Emilio harm him when she had agreed to cooperate? It didn't make sense.

Pablo couldn't answer. His mouth was awash with cookies and milk. Anna shredded the corner of the report card. He stared at her and swallowed hastily.

"Mama, my report card!" he cried.

"Sorry," she said. She laid the card on the table. "Pablo, *why* didn't you see Luis today?" It was an effort to keep her voice under control.

"Maybe he had practice, Mama." Pablo reached for another cookie. Anna shook her head and he pulled back, unabashed.

"No, today is your soccer day," she said. "Didn't he tell you he'd be late?" There had been plenty of time for Emilio to send someone to pick Luis up from school. Maybe he wanted to be absolutely sure of her.

Pablo frowned. "Mama!"

Before he could protest any further, Luis opened the kitchen door. Anna closed her eyes and said a silent prayer of thanks. Luis took one look at his mother's face and stopped short.

"Mama, are you all right?" he said.

"Course she's all right," said Pablo. "Don't be dumb." He jumped up from the table and ran upstairs.

Luis kissed his mother. She clutched at his sleeve, then patted it. She swallowed her fears and laughed, giddy with relief.

"Everything's fine," she said in a light tone. "Now how was school today?"

He looked at her uncertainly, then sat down at the kitchen table.

"School was okay. Sorry I was late, Mama, I had to drop off Julian's books before coming home." He reached into the cookie jar. "Where's Papa?"

"He was sent out of town." It wasn't any easier lying to Luis. Anna got up and went to the refrigerator.

"Where did he go?"

"He wasn't allowed to tell me," Anna said. She handed him the fresh pitcher of milk and a glass, then took Pablo's empty glass over to the sink. "I'm sure we'll hear from him soon." She wished she believed it. "You'll just have to be the man of the family till he gets back." She ruffled his silky, black hair, and didn't respond to his bewildered expression. She didn't want to think about his expression if he knew the truth.

Pablo tore back into the kitchen in his soccer uniform. She wiped off his milk mustache with a dishtowel. "I'm ready, Mama," he said, squirming.

"Do you want to come with us?" she asked Luis.

"Thanks, Mama, I'd rather study," he said. "We have a geography test tomorrow."

"All right, but be sure to lock the door after us," she instructed. "And don't open it to any strangers -

don't open it to anyone." Luis stared at her. She knew she had overdone the concern and kissed the top of his head. "Sorry. We'll see you later, querida."

Chapter Four

July 11, 1988

Anna was waiting downstairs when the doorbell rang. She wasn't ready to face Emilio again, but the boys were upstairs and she needed some time alone to compose herself. The past twenty-four hours had been a merry-go-round of fear for Romo, terror for their sons, and panic at the prospect of this first dinner with Emilio. Only the merry-go-round wasn't very merry.

Emilio's secretary had called late yesterday to inform her, in a cool, impersonal voice, that she was not to worry about a sitter for the boys. Someone would be provided. The possibilities conjured up by that statement terrified her more than anything else.

Anna opened the door. Emilio stood next to a young woman who was dressed casually in black jeans and a red sweater that looked as if they'd been poured on to her model-like form. Her short blond hair had black roots.

She wondered why he was going out with her when he had this bombshell in tow? Or did he have her on the side as well?

"Please come in," said Anna. She held the door open, and Emilio stepped back to let the bombshell enter. He followed her, resplendent in a white dinner jacket and black tie, and leaned toward Anna. She quickly offered him her cheek. When he kissed her, the odor of sandalwood made her nostrils twitch.

"Anna, this is Juanita," he said, and turned to the bombshell. "Juanita, Anna Peregrino."

"Hello," said Anna.

"Good evening Anna." Juanita held out her hand. Anna responded reluctantly, and was surprised at the strength in Juanita's grip. Her voice was a surprise too, more pleasant than sexy. She wasn't what Anna expected. In a strange way, that frightened her more.

"Where are the boys?" Emilio asked. "They should meet Juanita before we go."

Anna nodded. She turned and called up the stairs, "Boys! Could you come down here please?"

Feet pounded along the hall above their heads. Pablo and Luis slowed slightly as they rounded the corner and tore down the stairs.

"Uncle Emilio!" Luis cried joyfully. Anna cringed. In her fear and her anger at Emilio, she had forgotten that Pablo and Luis still looked on him as family. Emilio

36

was oblivious to her reaction, but Juanita had a curious look on her face. Anna couldn't tell if she'd noticed.

"What did you bring us?" Pablo grabbed hold of Emilio's hand.

Emilio laughed and clapped both boys on the shoulder. "Yes, Pablo, I brought you something. I brought a friend to stay with you." He smiled at Pablo's disappointed look. "I think you'll like Juanita. She's very good at computer games."

"Mama!" shouted Pablo, "Can we use your computer tonight? Please?"

Even Luis was waiting hopefully, watching her. "For an hour," she said. "That's it." Their enthusiasm sickened her, but they had no reason to be unfriendly. "Behave yourselves," she said. "Bedtime at nine o'clock." The boys groaned.

Anna smoothed Luis' black hair. He reminded her of herself at twelve, aloof, observing. He had been doing that a lot lately. He was growing up.

"Why don't you show me upstairs?" Juanita said to the boys. Anna's heart sank as she watched the three of them climb the stairs. Pablo chattered freely, and even Luis was asking questions of their new acquaintance.

"I brought you this." Emilio's voice brought Anna back. He was holding out a corsage of white gardenias, smiling, anxious to please, even handsome. It was hard to believe this was the same man who had threatened her yesterday morning.

If I give you a present, you accept it, he had said. She took the corsage, her fingers brushing his.

"Thank you," she said. She forced a smile. "These are lovely."

"Almost as lovely as you," he murmured. She sniffed the heavy perfume of the flowers, trying not to choke.

Her hands were steady as she pinned the corsage on her dress. She pretended to admire it in the hall mirror. Instead of white gardenias she saw pink roses. The first flowers Romo had given her. She banished the thought, and turned to find Emilio taking in every inch of her black silk dress. It was the only dress she owned that was both flattering and demure. If they went out a lot, clothes were going to be a problem.

"Shall we go?" said Anna. She had plans for this evening. It was time to go to work.

"Bring the wine list." The waiter bowed and moved away and Emilio turned to Anna with a smile. In spite of a secluded table in a dark corner, Anna was acutely uncomfortable during her first public appearance with him.

"I think you'll find their food extraordinary, my dear."

"If it's up to your standards, I'm sure I'll enjoy it," she replied. The thought of food made her choke. "I remember some of the dishes you cooked for my parents." Emilio was a gourmet cook, and his meals had been the highlights of many family visits. His smile broadened.

"Your father liked my Sole Bonne Femme. He said it reminded him of your mother - the Good Wife!"

If only they were there now to see him - the Good Friend!

"Your mother, on the other hand, was a true

American. No matter the occasion, she always wanted me to grill hamburgers." Anna responded with a polite laugh, and Emilio beamed.

He was in a good mood. Now was the time to try.

"Emilio," Anna began. She stopped. Did she dare run the risk of upsetting him?

"Yes, my dear?"

"May I ask a question?"

"A question?"

"Yes, I -" Her apprehension communicated itself to him and impatience clouded his face. "I'm sorry," she said, "It's not important."

"What's not important?" His annoyed expression belied his silky voice. When she hesitated he snapped, "What?"

"I just wondered if you've seen Romo since yesterday, and -"

Emilio's hand snaked forward and pinned hers to the table. He leaned closer, smiling, and hissed, "Don't ever mention his name again in public. Do you understand?" She nodded.

She had blown it. He'd kill all of them.

It looked like such an intimate scene. His hand resting on hers, his distinguished silver head inclined toward her as he whispered. No outsider could have known that his grip was crushing her fingers, and that his voice conveyed menace, not affection. The waiter hovered discreetly a few feet away, apparently unwilling to intrude.

Emilio released her and beckoned to him.

Anna watched in disbelief while Emilio calmly accepted the wine list as if nothing had happened, and studied it.

"We'll start with champagne," he said.

"Yes sir."

"Dom Perignon." Emilio handed the wine list back. "We'll have oysters as an appetizer, then decide on dinner." Again the waiter bowed and retreated.

Anna decided to try another tack. She waited until the man was out of earshot and spoke earnestly. "Emilio, I'm sorry."

He waved her apology aside, but she continued.

"I *am* sorry, but I'm also concerned. Surely you can understand that?" He was looking at someone over her shoulder. She started to turn, curious.

"Don't move," he said. She stiffened. He nodded to the person behind her, and then turned his attention back to her. "I was not joking, Anna. You are not to bring up his name again. Do you understand?"

"Yes, but-"

"No buts," snapped Emilio. "You don't ask. You don't try to find out anything." His eyes narrowed slightly. "You haven't said anything to anyone, have you?"

"Of course not." Anna didn't hesitate to lie. One second of uncertainty and she knew Emilio would catch on. Heaven help her if he knew she had talked to Padre Vincent in church.

"Good. See that you don't." Emilio's urbane smile was still pasted to his face, in contrast to the deadly seriousness of his tone.

She didn't dare push him any further. They remained silent until the waiter returned with champagne. He skillfully popped the cork and poured two glasses. Emilio raised his glass to Anna.

"To the future." They touched glasses and drank. "I'm the envy of every man in this room," said Emilio with an ardent look. "You are lovely tonight, my dear."

It made her sick, but Anna knew she had to play along. She had already jeopardized everything by being too direct. Up until now she'd simply accepted his unwanted attentions. It was clear to her that she needed to work a lot harder to keep him from losing patience. She flashed Emilio a brilliant smile.

"Let me return the compliment," she said. "There isn't a woman here who wouldn't love to trade places with me and be dining with such a handsome gentleman." And she wished they could.

He puffed up like a peacock. Interesting. It didn't take much to keep his little fantasy going.

The waiter slid the oysters onto the table and disappeared without missing a beat. Emilio looked as if he wanted to smack his lips over the feast in front of him.

"Would you care for some oysters, my dear?" he asked. Without waiting for her to respond, he lifted several onto her plate. He served himself and saluted her. "Bon appetit, Anna."

Oysters were not her favorite food, but she picked up her fork. She almost gagged when Emilio slipped an oyster into his mouth and swallowed with a beatific smile. She averted her gaze and managed to choke down what was on her plate.

"More?"

Anna looked up to see Emilio offering her the remaining oysters with a grin.

"No, thank you," she said. "You go ahead."

"I think I will. I seem to have developed quite an appetite." His greedy eyes devoured her while he consumed one oyster after another.

Anna tried to quiet the panic rising inside. She knew he couldn't do anything in the middle of a crowded restaurant, and Juanita would be there when they got home. Then again, that might not matter.

A frown marred his expression. He was getting annoyed with her again. She couldn't afford that.

"What would you recommend for dinner, Emilio?" Flatter him. Keep him diverted.

"They make a wonderful chateaubriand," he said. His glance lingered on her lips. "We can share it."

She forced herself to smile teasingly. "Is that all you can suggest?"

"I have many other suggestions, my dear," he purred. "But they will have to wait until we know one another a little better."

Know one another better? Who was he kidding? It took every ounce of her willpower to keep smiling. She laid her hand over his.

"I can't wait," she replied softly.

Chapter Five

July 12, 1988

"I like Juanita," announced Pablo. He shoveled eggs into his mouth and gulped his milk.

"She's okay," said Luis, with a troubled expression. He drank his orange juice. "Mama, why was she here last night?"

Anna wrapped sandwiches, taking her time to respond. She had to handle this carefully.

"I had to go out last night," she said. "And you aren't old enough yet to be left alone at night."

"I wouldn't listen to you!" Pablo chimed in. Luis ignored his little brother.

"But usually Carmella or Fatima come over," he said. "Why did Uncle Emilio bring Juanita?"

Anna glanced at Luis. "Didn't you like her?" she asked. "I thought she could play computer games."

Pablo mumbled between bites of toast, "She was great!"

"She was fine, Mama. I liked her too. And she's very good at computer games." Luis pushed his plate away, his food untasted. "I just wondered."

"Are you both finished with breakfast?" At their nods she ordered, "Run up and brush your teeth." Pablo dashed out of the kitchen. Luis followed with a backward look at his mother.

Her heart ached over his confusion. Luis was too bright and too sensitive for his own good. Or hers. She turned back to the lunches and put a mango in each bag. What could she say to him? What if Emilio heard Luis asking questions? Her heart raced at the thought.

Anna took the lunch bags over to the table. She started to clear away the breakfast dishes, when she heard scuffling noises overhead. "Take it easy up there," she called. She carried dishes over to the sink while she debated what to do about Luis.

Pablo darted back into the kitchen. "Fix my shoes, Mama," he demanded in his childish treble. Luis followed him into the room at a slower pace. He and Anna exchanged amused glances. Pablo was always in too much of a hurry to learn how to do things for himself. She blinked back sudden tears. How could Romo even consider a divorce? Didn't he love his sons? Didn't he love her? She sighed. Did it matter, since he could be dead by now?

"Put your foot up on the chair," she said. Pablo shifted impatiently while she tied his sneakers. He gave her a hasty kiss, and bolted from the kitchen. She could hear him shouting at his friends outside.

"I have soccer practice after school, Mama," said Luis. "Could I have some money for the bus?"

"Go get my purse from upstairs," Anna said. Luis loped off to find his mother's bag. She wiped the table with a dishrag and thought about Pablo. How easy would it be for Emilio to turn Pablo's happy shouts to screams of terror?

"Mama, are you all right? You look upset." Anna looked up to find Luis watching her with concern.

She brushed a strand of hair from her forehead and smiled at him. "You worry too much, Luis. I'm fine." Relief flooded his face. She took the leather bag from him and found some change. He accepted it with a grateful kiss.

"I won't be too late."

"Be careful," she called to his disappearing back. Her shoulders slumped and she dropped into a chair. She was exhausted. One breakfast with her sons and she felt as if she'd run a marathon. She had never known how much energy it took to be on guard every minute. To smile and behave as if everything is all right when your world is falling apart.

The dishes were waiting in the sink. Anna didn't have the strength to face them. It wasn't just being tired. Every time she saw dishwater it reminded her of the aftermath of Romo's arrest. She wondered if she was going crazy.

She'd wondered that last night, too. From Emilio's behavior during dinner, she had been sure he expected to go to bed when they got back to the house. Instead, he left with Juanita. But he'd be back. Anna took a deep breath and got to her feet. It was time to attack the dishes.

'Once upon a time.' Anna read the words on her computer screen. What a joke. Life wasn't 'once upon a time'. Not now, anyway. Life had always been a bit of a fairy tale for Anna Kelly. She had met her handsome prince and they'd lived happily ever after. Until his arrest.

Anna got up and poured herself a cup of coffee. That fairy tale was a joke too. Romo had asked for a divorce. While tormented by thoughts of Romo's arrest and Emilio's threats, she was still haunted by the spectre of divorce. What could have been so awful that it drove him, a devout Catholic, to ask for a divorce? It couldn't be another woman. That was the one part of her marriage that was never a problem.

The telephone shrilled and her entire body tensed. Anna picked up the receiver. "Hello?" she said. Tomas' familiar growl sounded on the other end, and she relaxed. In addition to being Romo's closest friend since university days, Tomas acted as literary agent for both of them.

"Tomas, hi."

"Don't 'hi' me," he said. "You're late."

"No I'm not. The deadline you gave me is next week."

"Yeah. And usually I see a draft by now. What's up?"

Anna frowned at the monitor that displayed only the sentence fragment on its screen. "I told you I'd
46

have it ready. Don't be such a grouch."

"Don't try to sidetrack me." His voice came booming out of the phone. "How much have you written?"

"None of your business," she said. She was too busy for fairy tales these days.

"You're only on the first page aren't you?" he said.

"What if I am?"

"I knew it!" She heard a crash through the receiver.

"Tomas?" Anna strained to hear what was happening on the other end of the line. "Tomas, what's going on?" She heard him swearing in the background, then he spoke into the phone again.

"I knocked over a pile of books," he said. "It's all your fault."

"Forget that," Anna said, interrupting. "Listen, I need to ask you about something." He was silent. "Do you still have copies of all those articles Romo wrote last year - especially that series on South Africa?"

"Why?" She was surprised to hear a note of caution in his voice. Tomas usually spoke first and thought later. That was one of the reasons he and Romo had become fast friends at university - brothers of impulse.

"I don't know," Anna evaded. "I thought I'd read some of his stuff while he's away."

"He's away?"

"Yeah. On assignment."

"Where?" asked Tomas.

"I don't know. He couldn't tell me."

Silence. "Umm. I'll have to look around." He coughed. "Can't you get all those articles from Romo's files or Emilio's files?"

"No. Not right now," she said.

"How long will he be gone?"

"He didn't know."

"Funny. Romo usually lets me know when he's going out of town. Wonder why he didn't call this time?"

"How would I know?" snapped Anna.

"Sorry, sorry, just thought I'd ask."

She regretted her flash of temper. If anyone knew why Romo had been arrested, it would be Tomas. She had to try to pump him without letting on that anything was wrong.

"Sorry Tomas, the boys were especially wild this morning." She sipped her cold coffee. "By the way, did Romo mention some sort of trouble to you?"

"Trouble?" he said. "What do you mean?"

"You know - did he talk to you about anything that was going on? Was he bothered by-" She stopped. What if Tomas was in on it too? Or what if Juanita had tapped her phone last night? If she had, it was already too late.

"You mean was Romo in trouble?" asked Tomas. Without waiting for her answer he continued. "He never said anything to me. Why do you ask?"

"Oh, I don't know." Anna looked over at the marked-up manuscript still sitting in the middle of Romo's desk. She wondered if Juanita had read it. Not that there was anything to learn from it. "He was in a bad mood right before he left."

"You mean you two were fighting again." It was a statement, not a question.

Tomas always took Romo's side. Did he know Romo wanted a divorce? Anna forced herself to stay calm and stick to the subject. This was no time to scream at someone who might have information. "Tomas," she said in a wheedling tone of voice. "You're Romo's best friend. Wouldn't he tell you if he were upset about something?"

"You're his wife," he countered. "Wouldn't he tell you?"

"Don't be rude. That's none of your business."

"No, but your work is." Tomas sounded unruffled and businesslike. "I want to see you tomorrow, draft in hand."

"Don't hold your breath!" Anna slammed the receiver down. Either Tomas really didn't know anything, or he wasn't telling. She'd find a way to figure out which. She'd call Maria.

"Maria, I'm over here!" Anna waved to Tomas' wife, a small, dark girl who was hovering at the entrance to the indoor garden restaurant. Maria smiled and waved back. She wove her way through the wrought iron tables scattered among the greenery on the flagstone patio.

Did she know anything? Would Tomas have confided in her? Maria puzzled her. Tomas had married Maria shortly after Luis was born. In fact, immediately after he had played godfather at Luis' baptism, Tomas left town and came back married.

Anna often wondered why she didn't get along better with Maria. They seemed to have a lot in common - Maria wrote for a university publication, she'd travelled a great deal; their husbands were best friends. The four of them went out to dinner occasionally, but Tomas seemed to prefer meeting Romo and she alone. Still, Maria was his wife, and if anyone knew Tomas' business, she should.

"Hello Anna," said Maria. The two women brushed cheeks. "How are you?"

"Fine, I'm fine thanks," Anna replied. "How are you? I see Tomas all the time but the four of us never seem to be able to get together." They sat down and Anna motioned the waiter to bring the menus.

"I'm fine, but a little busy. Deadlines." Maria shook her dark bangs out of her face. "I had to do some fast talking at the university to be able to meet you on such short notice." She looked at Anna quizzically. The waiter reappeared next to their table and filled the water glasses.

"Shall we order?" asked Anna. They gave the waiter their orders, and when he left Maria spoke.

"So, Anna, why did you want to see me?"

Anna smiled brightly. "I just thought it had been too long since we had seen each other. We never get a chance to talk." She took a sip of her water.

"Yes," agreed Maria, "And it must be lonely now with Romo on assignment."

Anna choked on the water. Maria's eyebrows flew up. Anna coughed and took another sip. "Sorry. How did you know Romo was gone? He just left yesterday."

"I talked to Tomas this morning. Right before

you called, in fact." She touched the petals of the rose in the centerpiece. "Why? Shouldn't he have told me?"

Anna caught Maria watching her while pretending to be absorbed in the rose. She had to be careful. Maria already seemed to be too suspicious.

"No, it's no secret," said Anna. "I was surprised he'd talked to you that soon, that's all."

"Well, he is my husband." Maria's voice had an edge to it. She seemed to hear it, and moderated her tone. "Tomas told me they sent him off with no notice and you don't know when he'll be in touch."

Anna sighed. "It's especially hard on Pablo and Luis. They hate to come home and find their father gone."

"It must have been a shock," Maria sympathized. "Sometimes when he sees those boys of yours I think Tomas regrets not having children." Anna saw a flicker of anger cross Maria's face so quickly that a second later she doubted she had even seen it.

"There's still plenty of time," she assured her. "You and Tomas are still young."

Maria shook her head. "No, Tomas doesn't want children."

"I don't understand," said Anna. "He loves Pablo and Luis. He plays with them every time he comes over."

"That's because they're *your* children," said Maria. Anna wondered at the emphasis, but the waiter came with their salads before she could ask.

"I see what you're saying." Anna continued the conversation after the waiter left. "Some people love other people's children, but don't want the responsibility of their own."

"Right," replied Maria in a dry voice. She focused her attention on the shrimp in front of her and began to eat.

Anna toyed with the leafy spinach on her plate while she watched Maria.She had to find out if Maria knew what was going on. Tomas might have told his wife something he wouldn't tell her.

"Maria, is everything all right with Tomas and Romo?"

Maria's head jerked up. "What do you mean?"

Anna tried to choose her words carefully. "I wondered if they were still working as closely together before Romo left. You know, what they were working on, was everything okay."

Maria's look of amazement told her she had been too blunt. She'd have to try something else.

"Actually, Maria," she confided, "Romo and I had been fighting a lot before he went away. He wasn't talking to me much, and I wondered if Tomas had said anything."

"Not about the two of you," said Maria.

"About anything?" Anna jumped in. Maria's eyes narrowed and Anna tried to cover herself. "I'm worried about him. I thought Tomas might have mentioned something."

"You'd have to ask Tomas, wouldn't you?" suggested Maria. Her cheeks were spots of bright red, and she laid down her fork. "You and my husband are such great friends, why don't you ask him?"

Anna reeled at the hostility in Maria's voice. They'd always been friendly, if not close. What was the source of this antagonism?

"Maria, I'm sorry." Anna tried to salvage their lunch. "I was only hoping we could talk, and I thought you and Tomas might have-"

"No, Anna," Maria said, interrupting with a glare at her. "I'm sorry." Any pretense of friendship had vanished, and Anna stared at her. "The truth is, I haven't been feeling too well lately. Would you please excuse me?"

Without waiting for Anna's response, Maria rose, picked up her purse, and stalked out of the restaurant. Anna was stunned. This animosity was a side of Maria she'd never seen. She didn't know what to think.

The waiter came to take her money, and Anna tried to ignore the ever-present panic inside. No one seemed to know anything about what had happened to Romo. No one had any ideas about what he might have been involved in before his arrest. No one could or would tell her anything. And Emilio would be expecting her to go out with him again. Soon.

July 13, 1988

Anna tried to open the door to Tomas' office. It stuck at the halfway point, stopped by a heavy cardboard box. Stacks of books adorned the window sills and chairs of the office, while manila folders and assorted papers cluttered the rest of the landscape, which consisted of little more than a desk and two bookcases.

Tomas sat behind the desk, his bulky frame bent over an open book. Anna could only see the top of his head, its wiry salt and pepper hair thinning at the crown. She tossed a large envelope on top of the mess in front of Tomas. "There's your draft."

He looked up at her over bifocals that perched on the bridge of an impressive nose. "Thanks," he said. He opened the envelope and glanced at the pages, then started to read. Anna stood across the desk from him and marveled at how easily he was caught up in her story. That was one of the reasons he was a good agent, he loved to read.

"Good thing you don't neglect your office the way you neglect your clients," said Anna. "Can't you even say hello?"

Tomas chuckled. He put down the papers and took off the glasses. It was an old argument between them. "Hello," he said, "And I'll clean tomorrow. I promise." He came out from behind the desk, arms outstretched for a hug. Anna kissed him on the cheek, but held him at arm's length. A crease appeared between his brows, and he searched her eyes. Anna knew he could see nothing. She had learned a lot about hiding her feelings the last few days. But, she still had a lot to learn about getting information without giving any.

"Don't clean on my account," she said, stepping back and smiling. "It wouldn't be your office without the tornado effect."

He chuckled. "One of these days I'll shock you and get organized." Anna caught him watching her surreptitiously while he took a stack books off the seat of a red leather armchair.

Maria must have told him about their lunch. Or was her behavior giving her away?

Tomas tossed the books into a cardboard box

and motioned toward the chair. Anna checked for stray rubbish, then sat down.

"So, how are you, Anna?" he said. He perched on the corner of the desk, his dusty desert boot swinging inches from the folds of her black skirt.

"Fine, thanks." She shifted far enough in the chair to move her skirt out of danger. "Why were you in such a big hurry for that draft?"

"Don't want you to miss the deadline," he said. Tomas pulled out a pack of cigarettes. He held it out to her and she refused. "Hear from Romo?" His attention appeared to be on the cigarette he was lighting.

"Not yet."

"Really? I'd have thought he'd call by now."

"Nope. Have you heard from him?" said Anna. She couldn't trust him. What if he was in on it with Emilio?

"Me? Why would he call me and not you?"

"You never know." Anna's voice was even. "You're his best friend."

Tomas regarded his cigarette with a frown. "And you're his wife."

"Let's not get into that again." The words were out before Anna could stop herself. She took a deep breath and met Tomas' penetrating stare with a calm demeanor. "He did say it might be a while before I'd hear from him." Tomas stubbed out his cigarette in the overflowing ashtray on the desk.

"Too bad." He hopped off the corner of the desk and went round to his chair. He sat down, a serious look on his face. "I had someone who was interested in his work. They have a deadline soon, though."

"Sorry," she said. "Can't help you." Anna picked up a paperback lying on the chair next to her and leafed through it. "Did you have him working on any other projects, Tomas?"

His shoulders stiffened. She pretended to be absorbed by the book. He knows something, she thought. I knew it - he and Romo tell each other everything.

"Not that I recall," he said. "Why?"

Anna gripped the paperback tight. Her knuckles whitened. Why was Tomas asking leading questions? Did he want to know what she knew? Or was he trying to find out where Romo was? Or was he working with Emilio and just testing her? Whatever the reason, he wasn't going to find out one damn thing.

"No reason," she said, looking up and smiling at him. "You know Romo. He gets buried in his work. Sometimes he takes on more than he can handle."

Tomas relaxed and leaned back in his chair. "What *is* this new assignment?"

"I don't know," she said. "Romo gets so touchy when I ask questions." Tomas raised an eyebrow. "All right, he and I don't always agree on his priorities."

"Yes," he said dryly, "I remember."

If he knew anything about a divorce he wasn't talking about it. Anna laid the paperback on the chair beside her and stood up. "I have things to do, Tomas." She stood in front of his desk, her purse on her shoulder, ready to leave. "Is there anything else?"

"Yes," he said. Anna waited for him to continue. "That was nice of you to call Maria for lunch yesterday." Anna couldn't tell from his expression whether or not Maria had told him how they parted.

"We had a nice time," she said cautiously. A muscle twitched in Tomas' cheek, but he smiled.

"You haven't seen each other in a long time. Why the sudden interest in Maria?"

"You said it," Anna replied, fencing. "I hadn't seen her in a while."

"What did you two find to talk about?" There was a sarcastic edge to his words. Anna was sure he was worried about something. But what?

"Girl talk, Tomas. It wouldn't interest you."

"You'd be surprised," he said. His face was guileless, but Anna didn't believe him for a second. He knew something. If only she could trust him. But after what Emilio had said last night, there was no way she'd take that chance.

"Thanks." Her chin lifted. "I appreciate your interest."

His brows contracted and he opened his mouth to speak, but she forestalled him.

"Let me know how you like the story." She spun on her heel and turned back to wave at him from the door. "And give my love to Maria." She walked out.

Chapter Six

July 19, 1988

"Eduardo, I'd like you to meet Anna Peregrino." Emilio ushered a short, round man in to the symphony box, where Anna was seated on a gilt chair. She gritted her teeth and smiled. Eduardo waddled forward to kiss her hand. She wanted to snatch it away, but instead, submitted gracefully. His fingers were pudgy, like the rest of him, and his palm was damp. Perspiration glistened on the top of his bald head.

"Anna, this is one of my business associates, Eduardo Lucas." Emilio's ramrod posture telegraphed to her the importance of this visitor, and she obediently murmured a greeting.

"You didn't tell me how lovely she was, Emilio."

At his oily tone, Anna cringed inside. She met Eduardo's lascivious smirk with polite attention. Emilio was unpredictable. She didn't want to appear rude, but she had no desire to encourage Eduardo.

"Yes, she is quite a beauty," Emilio agreed. "We've known one another since Anna was a child, isn't that right my dear?"

"Yes, that's right," said Anna.

"I envy you." Eduardo turned to grin at Emilio. "Let me know if there's anything I can do for you. Maybe we can exchange favors sometime?"

A chill swept through Anna. Would Emilio use her to trade favors? She swallowed the lump in her throat. He couldn't do that, she thought desperately, Not with that pig. A quick look at Emilio's expressionless face gave no hint to his thoughts.

Emilio gestured at the box next to theirs. "Isn't that your wife waving at us?" Eduardo returned the wave impatiently, and Emilio bowed from the waist.

"It was quite a pleasure to meet you, Anna," said Eduardo. She allowed him to take her hand again and press his lips to her flesh. Emilio frowned behind Eduardo's back. His frown was transformed to a smile when Eduardo turned around. Anna could hear the rumble of their voices when Emilio escorted his guest into the foyer.

The red velvet curtains parted silently and Emilio returned to his seat at her side. "Very nice, Anna," he said, "You handled him quite well."

"Thank you." And you can go to hell, she thought.

"It should be an excellent program tonight. They're playing Liszt and Chopin in the first half."

59

"What pieces?" she asked. It didn't interest her, but she thought it was safer to keep him talking.

"I believe the Chopin is a piano concerto." He consulted his program. "Yes, and the Liszt is "Les Preludes"."

A prelude to what? Was the concert the prelude to the rest of the evening? Emilio chatted about the music while he scanned the other boxes for influential acquaintances.

Anna covertly observed him. How much power and influence did he have? Would he be able to keep her to himself even if someone like Eduardo decided he wanted her? She shivered at the memory of his greedy expression. And what would happen if Emilio did keep her to himself? So far he'd been a gentleman. It was difficult to believe that state of affairs would last.

Emilio noticed her scrutiny. His shoulders straightened and his chest puffed out. Anna reddened. She studied her program book, aware that he interpreted her blushing as shyness, not anger at being caught watching. His vanity made it easy for her to play her part.

The conductor started for the podium, and the audience applauded. Anna clapped too. It might be a game, but it was one she could not afford to lose. Her applause became wild, as if the sound could drown out the clamor of her fears.

The applause died and the house lights brightened. Anna watched the musicians straggling off the stage. She felt Emilio's eyes on her, but tried to ignore him as long as possible.

He leaned close. "Anna-" The curtains at the

back of the box parted and Eduardo entered with another man beside him. Emilio rose instantly, his hand under Anna's elbow, raising her with him.

"Emilio, I brought someone who is anxious to meet you and your beautiful guest." Anna glanced at the man towering over Eduardo. Even Emilio looked short by comparison. He looked familiar, but she couldn't quite place him. Eduardo introduced them. "This is Emilio Carrera and Anna Peregrino, Diego. Emilio, Anna, Diego Belen, one of the most successful businessmen in Santiago."

Of course, she had seen him on the news and in the papers many times. He was one of the few businessmen Romo had admired.

"How do you do, Señorita Peregrino?" Diego bent over her hand with a grace that shamed his companion.

"Señora Peregrino," said Anna. She cast a swift glance at Emilio to see if her correction had made him angry. His face was like carved stone, and her heart sank.

"I beg your pardon," Diego apologized. He turned to Emilio and shook his hand. "Señor Carrera, a pleasure."

"Are you enjoying the concert Anna?" asked Eduardo.

"Yes, very much," said Anna. She tried to edge away as Eduardo sidled toward her, but there was little room to maneuver in the crowded box.

"Eduardo, perhaps Señora Peregrino would like a glass of wine?" Diego spoke in a soft voice, but the command was implicit. Eduardo instantly left the box. "You are a widow, then, Señora?"

Anna looked at him, startled. "No, my husband is a journalist. He's away on an assignment." Emilio smoothly picked up the conversation.

"I was a close friend of Anna's parents," he said. "I've known her since she was a child, and her husband writes for my magazine."

Diego raised his eyebrows. "Then your husband is Romulo Peregrino?"

"Yes," said Anna. She lifted her chin.

"He's a fine writer. You must be very proud of him." Surprised by his praise, she swallowed convulsively. Eduardo bustled through the curtains with a waiter behind him, providing a needed distraction.

"I am," she replied softly. Emilio didn't hear her response, but Diego nodded in silent agreement.

The waiter served each of them a glass of wine and left. Eduardo lifted his glass in a toast. "To you, Anna, a vision of loveliness." They all drank and he turned to Emilio, raising his glass again, "And to favors, my friend." Anna stood frozen while the three men drank.

"And why to favors, Eduardo?" asked Diego. He had moved slightly so that Eduardo could not get close to Anna without displacing him. Eduardo's discomfiture seemed to amuse him and he smiled while he waited for an answer.

"It's nothing," said Eduardo. "Just a private joke." He leered at Anna from the other end of the box, but did not object when Diego said it was time to go. Diego herded him through the curtains without letting him get near Anna, then turned back to her briefly.

"Don't worry Señora Peregrino, he won't bother you again." He disappeared through the curtains. Anna was afraid to look at Emilio. She knew he'd missed none of the byplay in the box. Finally, she glanced over at his straight figure.

Emilio's face was ashen. His lips were white with rage, and he slashed at her, "You disloyal bitch!"

"What?" Anna was dumbfounded. Her heart raced. "I thought you *wanted* me to be polite to your friends."

"Polite! Do you call fawning all over him being polite?"

"Who? Diego?"

"Yes, Diego," he mocked. "And he isn't my friend! Nor is he likely to be." Anna was aghast at the torrent of words pouring out of Emilio. She had never known this man at all, in spite of the number of years they had been acquainted. She had to calm him or she could be in serious trouble.

"Can't we sit down," she said. "You're attracting attention."

He ignored her suggestion. "You seem to like attention, my dear." He was still visibly upset, but his voice had quieted.

"Emilio, I'm sorry," she protested. "Believe me, I was only trying to please you. I have no interest in anyone else. I was doing what I thought you wanted me to do."

Color came back to his face while he listened to her words. He reached out to touch her hair, his hand trembling. "Forgive me Anna. Of course you were trying to please me." He stroked her hair gently, and she had to suppress a shudder. "It wasn't your fault."

It wasn't anyone's fault, she thought, because

it wasn't anything. A man was simply trying to be a gentleman. How to settle him down? She took his hand in both of hers, her skin crawling at the unwelcome contact. "Let's sit down. It's time for the second half of the concert." The lights had dimmed and she could see Eduardo and his party watching them from the next box. Emilio held Anna's chair for her, then sat beside her.

"It will be just the two of us from now on," he whispered. As the first notes of a Mozart concerto wafted into the house, Anna tried to relax. Emilio was so jealous. He lost control so easily. How could she keep him at arm's length, yet satisfy him and protect her husband and sons? If she had to err, it had better be on the side of keeping him happy. She tucked her hand into the crook of his arm. He smiled down at her and she tightened her grip, smiling back.

"The boys were fine," reported Juanita. Anna only half listened, aware of Emilio at her shoulder. She tried to figure out Emilio's next move. So far, he'd kept his distance, but after his swift anger at the symphony she felt herself to be on shaky ground. She tried to catch a glimpse of his expression, to see if she could read his intentions. "-was that okay?" Anna was jerked back to reality by Juanita's voice.

"Sorry," she said. "I guess I'm a little tired. Was what okay?"

"The three of us played computer games till late." Juanita looked at her strangely. "They said it was all right since they're on school holiday this week."

"Oh, sure," Anna said. "That's just fine." Emilio stirred impatiently. Her breath came faster.

"If you two are finished, let's get going Juanita."

Anna almost fainted with relief. She kept repeating Thank you, God, to herself, like a litany, while Emilio kissed her on the cheek, and followed Juanita out the door. It clicked shut and she collapsed into one of the kitchen chairs. She couldn't handle this alone any more. Tomorrow she would find a way to talk with Tomas.

Chapter Seven

July 20, 1988

"Remind you of your childhood?"

Anna wheeled at the sound of Tomas' voice, to find him grinning at her from behind the jungle gym. They were alone in the park. The gloomy, windy afternoon had kept the children at home.

"I thought you were the one who never wanted to grow up," Anna retorted. "You do look a little like Peter Pan. You know, green suit, green face."

"Don't be rude," said Tomas. "Why did you want to see me here instead of at the office?"

Anna perched on a nearby swing. "Oh, I don't

know." She pushed off and pumped the swing higher. "I thought it might be fun."

"Without Pablo and Luis? Come on Anna, what's going on?" Tomas stepped in front of her and caught the chains of the swing. It rocked crazily for a minute, and then subsided. She blinked.

"You're not much fun today Tomas. What's the matter?"

"Why are you asking me?" He glared down at her and abruptly released the swing. "You wanted to see me."

Anna's sneakers scuffed at the dirt hollow under the swing. The moment of truth. She was going to tell him about Romo. She had to trust someone. She drew a design in the dirt with the toe of her shoe. "I wanted-"

"Why did you have lunch with Maria?" He grasped the swing again, trapping Anna. His aggressive posture belied the quiet tone of his words.

"I told you," she said, startled by his combative behavior. "I hadn't seen her for a long time."

Tomas shook his head impatiently. "Not good enough. You were asking her some strange questions and I want to know why."

Anna slipped off the swing and under his arm. Something was wrong. He was acting suspicious of her. Could he be in on it with Emilio? Maybe Emilio told him to find out whether or not she'd talk if he pressured her enough. She wandered over to the wooden merry-go-round and started to push it. The safest thing would be to keep him off balance. The ancient toy groaned in protest but Anna pushed faster and faster. She hopped on the platform, hair flying out behind her.

"Come on, loosen up," she called, whirling past him. He stalked over and grabbed the railing. The merry-go-round came to an abrupt halt. Anna jumped off and staggered a few feet from the momentum. "What's with you? I could have been hurt," she said. He confronted her, his fists balled inside his pockets.

"Stop the games, Anna."

"What games?" She stiffened.

"That's enough!" Tomas grasped her arm above the elbow and propelled her back toward the merry-go-round. He sat down on the edge and pulled her down beside him. "You've been acting strange ever since Romo went away. Now what's going on?"

"Did Romo tell you he wanted a divorce?"

"From you?"

"No, from you," she snapped. "Of course from me. Did he tell you?" Anna already knew the answer from Tomas' expression, which looked as if she'd kicked him in the stomach.

"No," he said. "He didn't say a word. When did this happen?"

"The day he was- the day he left." Anna's mind raced. If Romo hadn't trusted Tomas enough to tell him about wanting a divorce, maybe there was a reason. Maybe he knew something about Tomas she didn't.

"Did he say why he wanted a divorce?"

"No."

"Why not?" said Tomas, staring at her.

Anna tried to see through his stare and read his thoughts. She couldn't tell. She couldn't tell if she could trust him. What if she did and it was the wrong choice? She studied his face, the face of an old friend. Just like Emilio. She couldn't risk it. Not yet.

"Sorry pal," she said with an effort. "I don't know any more."

Tomas sighed and cocked an eyebrow at her. "Then what did you think I could tell you?"

"I don't know," said Anna. She could tell that something didn't ring true to Tomas. It was time to get out of there.

Tomas rested his head on his hands, as if suddenly tired. "And we couldn't do this by phone?"

"You need to get out more often." She tried to recapture the light touch, but it eluded her. "I have to go. See you later." A few yards away, she looked back and he was still sitting there, head in hands, staring at the ground. I'm sorry, Tomas, she pleaded silently. But I'm not sure of you. And I can't afford to make a mistake.

Chapter Eight

July 27, 1988

Anna's eyes stung from the haze of smoke drifting through the nightclub. It was difficult to breathe. She wasn't sure if it was the effect of the smoke or of her companion.

Emilio sat across the cocktail table. She could feel his heated gaze on her as she looked around the club. He'd been like this all night. It was as if a furnace inside him were being stoked higher and higher, until finally Anna would be consumed by his desire. It hadn't helped that she'd worn one of her sexiest dresses. She hadn't realized the effect simple white jersey with a V-neck would have on him. Her nerves had been wound tight as the night wore on. Maybe she could distract him with conversation.

"It was a wonderful production, Emilio," she said. "The acting was excellent."

"Yes, I enjoyed it. I've always been partial to Tennessee Williams and this is one of his better plays." He finally looked away from her when the waitress came to take their order. "Brandy please, for both of us." It was too short a reprieve. He turned back to Anna, and her breath caught in her throat at the intensity of his look.

"I didn't realize you liked the theatre so much," she said hurriedly.

"It depends. There are some great works out there, but I don't care for many of the recent plays." He settled back in his chair to pontificate further. "I like to see a good story on the stage, not be bored by some idiot's political theories. That kind of work is stupid and dangerous."

Anna breathed an inward sigh of relief as he continued to rail against the modern political playwrights. At last he was intent on something other than her.

Going to see CAT ON A HOT TIN ROOF had not been her idea. Until tonight, Emilio had made no sexual demands. That had both surprised and relieved her. Watching him watch Maggie's attempts to seduce Brick had made her wonder if her luck had run out. She had worried about its effect on Emilio, and not without reason.

She nodded and smiled while he continued his monologue. Necessity had made her adept, in these last few weeks, at encouraging Emilio up to a point.

Necessity had taught her to keep him happy, yet stay one step ahead of him. Tonight looked like it might be a different story.

The waitress came back with their drinks. Emilio stopped talking while they sipped the brandy. The five-man combo on the tiny stage swung into a medley of Gershwin music. Emilio liked American things - Tennessee Williams, George Gershwin, her. He held out his hand.

"Dance?" It was not an invitation, and Anna responded to his command. It was the first time since Romo's arrest that Emilio had held her. He had touched her, kissed her, but not held her. She wanted to recoil. Instead she slid into his arms.

It was impossible to keep him at a distance. He drew her tightly against him with unyielding strength. They were both excellent dancers and Anna followed his lead easily. She felt suffocated by his proximity, his face too close, his body engulfing hers. Closing her eyes, she laid her head on his shoulder. At least she wouldn't have to look at him. And it would make him feel good.

One tune blended into another. Anna prayed for the band to take a break, but they played an endless parade of romantic music. Emilio pressed her intimately against him. She tried to lift her head and pull away, but he held her immobile. Imprisoned in his embrace she could feel the heat of his body through their clothing.

She almost screamed when he began to nuzzle her neck. Her fingers were like ice. She was sure Emilio could hear the pounding of her heart.

She shuddered as he breathed into her ear. He whispered, "Would you like to get out of here?"

"Yes," she choked. He kept one arm tight around her as they walked off the dance floor. Emilio tossed a large bill on the table, picked up her purse, and swept her out of the nightclub.

"The boys are fine," said Juanita.

"Thanks." Anna managed a smile for the babysitter. Thank heaven the evening was almost over. Emilio would go and she would be left alone. Anna's smile disappeared when Emilio helped Juanita with her jacket, and then took off his own.

"Tell Jose to drive you home. Then he's to come back and wait for me," he ordered. Juanita glanced at Anna, then looked away.

"Good night Anna," she said. She went out the front door. "Good night Emilio."

Emilio's good night was cheery as he closed the door behind her. Anna tried to hide her agitation.

"Would you like some coffee?" She started toward the kitchen without waiting for an answer. Emilio caught her arm.

"You know what I want," he muttered, drawing her toward the stairs. She stumbled on the first step. With an iron grip he prevented her from falling, and forced her to climb the stairs beside him. At the top of the stairs his grasp shifted to her hand. He led her into the bedroom.

Emilio let go of Anna and took off his jacket. She froze. He couldn't mean it. He couldn't really expect her to sleep with him. He took off his belt, unzipped his pants and looked at her. He said quietly, "Don't keep me waiting, Anna."

I can't let him touch me, she thought. He was her father's best friend, her husband's friend. She thought she might throw up. She took a deep breath and unzipped her dress. Emilio stopped undressing to watch her. She held the dress in front of her and stood, shivering in her slip.

"Don't stop now, Anna, keep going." His voice was hoarse. He nodded as she removed her slip. She didn't dare pause before taking off the rest. She tried to cover herself, but he drew her arms aside. He looked.

Standing there naked she thought, you bastard, how dare you do this to me. She didn't say it. She didn't say anything. Romo's life depended on her cooperation. And her children, so vulnerable and so close. She'd be damned if she'd betray that trust.

Once Emilio had looked his fill, he gestured toward the bed. Anna lay down. He removed his shorts and climbed on top of her. Her eyes fixed on the crucifix over the door.

Where was God now?. All those miracles in the Bible. Why wasn't there one for her? Emilio was telling her what to do. She followed his instructions, but it wasn't her. She could feel his insistent hands and the weight of his body. Only she wasn't there. It had nothing to do with her.

Her eyes never left the cross. She focused her rage and fear and pain on the two strips of wood glued together, and the twisted body on top. Finally he finished. Anna closed her eyes when he rolled off of her. A few minutes later his breathing was slow and rhythmic. She didn't move, barely breathed for fear of waking him. When one hour, then another passed, she wondered how to get him out before the boys got up.

Anna opened her eyes and checked the clock next to the bed. Two-thirty. It seemed much later, but they'd come home early. Emilio stirred next to her. She closed her eyes again and listened as he got up and dressed. She didn't move.

He was at the door when she looked up. "I'll call you in a day or so," he said. She still didn't move. Emilio's face darkened. "Don't forget your husband. Your sons. I'd like a kiss goodbye."

She got up from the bed and went to him. She couldn't smile. She couldn't kiss him on the lips. She had managed to avoid that so far. She felt like a whore. Maybe the actions of a whore would distract him from his kiss.

Anna whispered, "Close your eyes." He grinned and closed his eyes. Anna took a deep breath. With her left hand she pulled open his partially buttoned shirt and teased his right nipple with her tongue. At the same time her right hand deftly unzipped his fly and slipped inside to massage his penis.

He was immediately hard in her hand. She never looked up to see if his eyes had opened. Her mouth moved from one nipple to the other, first licking, then sucking. She had both hands inside his pants. Her right stroked and kneaded his penis to the rhythm of his groans. The nails of her left hand lightly raked his testicles. His climax was quick and intense.

He stood in the middle of the room, panting, eyes still closed. Anna took some tissues from the nightstand and wiped up the semen carefully. She refastened his pants and buttoned his shirt. His eyes were open. He looked sated, almost drugged. She stood in front of him, still naked, and waited.

"Good night, Anna," he said. His voice was

unsteady. "I'll call you tomorrow - today." He leaned his hand against the doorway for a second, then left. She didn't move.

The front door slammed. Anna grabbed a perfume bottle off the dresser and hurled it at the crucifix. Then she bolted into the bathroom and vomited into the toilet. She knelt, weeping and retching over the bowl until she was exhausted.

After what seemed like hours, there were no tears left to cry. Nothing left to throw up. She leaned back against the wall, sitting naked on the bathroom floor. It was cold. She was cold. Outside. Inside.

She felt covered in filth. She had to scrub it off. She didn't want anything of that bastard to cling to her.

Anna stepped into the shower and turned it on full blast. She turned around, and around again. The water cascaded all over her. It wasn't enough. She grabbed the soap and washcloth and lathered every inch of her body. It still didn't help.

She dove for the scrub brush under the sink. Water flew everywhere. She scrubbed her mouth to get rid of the taste of him. She barely noticed the foul taste of the soap. Anna scrubbed and scrubbed and scrubbed. Her skin was raw. She kept scrubbing.

It didn't work. She stayed in the shower for more than an hour and she wasn't clean. She had to get out, because Luis and Pablo might wake up and hear her. She wanted to stay in there forever.

Anna examined her body while she dried herself. Where were the bruises? Her shoulders, her thighs, her breasts. Nothing. She couldn't see anything. He had left no marks. Nothing visible.

He had said he'd call her today. Her stomach

heaved again at the thought. She knew she couldn't fight him. She couldn't argue. She couldn't do anything.

Anna reluctantly returned to the bedroom. Broken bits of the perfume bottle lay scattered under the crucifix. The scent of the perfume was heavy in the air. Circling the bed, Anna dug into Romo's dresser drawers. She pulled out his old gray sweat suit and put it on. She wouldn't look at the bed. If she didn't look at it, it couldn't hurt. She didn't feel anything. She didn't want to feel anything.

Anna checked to be sure the alarm was set. The boys had soccer camp. She rooted around in the bottom of the cedar chest at the foot of the bed, and unearthed a tattered patchwork quilt. She held it to her face. Her parents had laughed when she had asked for the quilt, but it was a part of her childhood. Wherever they moved, whatever country they visited, the quilt was there, at the foot of her parents' bed. Anna wrapped herself tightly in the quilt and lay down on the floor to try to sleep.

Chapter Nine

July 28, 1988

"Breakfast is ready," Anna called from the kitchen. Her hand shook when she flipped the last of the empanadas out of the frying pan and onto the platter. The pastries were fried just the way Pablo and Luis liked them. Anna carried the platter clamped in both hands, and set it on the table. Wisps of steam curled around the edges as Anna scooped them onto the plates.

The spatula trembled in her grasp. "Damn!" She threw the spatula into the sink and carefully picked up the coffee mug on the table. A sip of the scalding brew momentarily calmed her. Coffee was all her stomach could handle. Eating was impossible. "Boys!" she shouted.

Pablo rushed into the kitchen with Luis close behind. "Sorry Mama," Luis said. They sat down and Pablo immediately bit into his pastry.

"Mmmm, ham and cheese," Pablo mumbled. "My favorite."

"Don't talk with your mouth full." Luis admonished him with a disgusted look. "Pig."

"Eat," Anna commanded. She bustled around them, straightening silverware and pouring milk. Her head throbbed. She hadn't thought it would be this hard. She couldn't look at either of them.

She escaped to the stove, picked up the dirty skillet and a bowl, and put them in the sink.

"Sit down, Mama," Pablo said.

"Aren't you eating with us?" Luis asked.

Anna turned on the water and started scrubbing the skillet. "Not this morning. I have too many things to do."

"What things?" Pablo said.

"Lots of things." She couldn't look at him. "I have to finish these dishes, pack your lunches-"

"You always do that stuff. Why-"

"Pablo, shut up and eat," Luis ordered.

"You're not the boss of me," said Pablo. He grabbed another empanada. Anna glanced at Luis to see if she'd given herself away, but he was bent over his plate.

She turned back to the sink, closed her eyes and said a quick prayer. She didn't want the boys to think she was mad at them.

"How about a special treat with your lunches today?" Anna wiped her hands on the towel and threw it over the dish rack. "Did I hear you say they had ice cream bars for sale at lunch time?" She took some change from the jar on the refrigerator.

Pablo jumped up from his chair and raced over to give her a hug. "Ice cream! In the middle of winter!" His arms encircled her waist in a tight squeeze. For a second she remembered the pressure of Emilio's arms around her. It was obscene.

"Pablo, don't!" she snapped. He looked up at her, his forehead puckered. She didn't have the energy to apologize or explain. Besides, what could she tell him? "Go upstairs and brush your teeth," she said. She replaced the change jar and Pablo left dragging his feet.

Luis looked at his mother, a puzzled expression on his face. Anna thought, *I cannot handle his questions this morning.* "Finish your breakfast, Luis," she said. She put his money on the table and sat down to finish her coffee.

"Mama, is something wrong?" he asked. She shook her head. Sometimes she wished he weren't so perceptive.

"No," she said. "What's planned for soccer camp today?"

"We're supposed to work on passing." Luis pushed his plate away. "Are you mad about Juanita?"

Anna couldn't breathe. He knew. How could he know?

"Mad about Juanita," she said. "No. Why?"

80

The boys had been sound asleep when she and Emilio got home last night. She'd have heard them if they'd been awake.

"She uses your computer a lot when she's here," Luis explained. "You get mad at us."

Anna began to breathe again. She didn't know why Juanita was always on the computer, and she didn't care, so long as the boys didn't know about Emilio. "No, I'm not mad at Juanita." She managed to smile at him. "Come on, you'd better get ready for camp."

Her smile seemed to reassure him. He grinned and disappeared upstairs. She buried her head in her arms. What next? Even the thought of food made her sick, and her son's hug reminded her of the man who had raped her. She couldn't let herself fall apart. Maybe it was time to talk to Tomas.

Anna forced herself to get to her feet. She took the rest of the dishes over to the sink. When she heard feet pounding down the stairs, she picked up the lunch bags.

"You two be good today," she said. She gave each of them a lunch and a quick kiss. Thank God they were leaving.

"Thanks Mama."

"Goodbye Mama."

The kitchen door slammed and she was alone.

"Thanks for coming, Tomas," Anna said. She took his arm. They walked through the pillared gates at the entrance to the park. The formality of the entrance was in striking contrast to the winding pathway they climbed. It was flanked by stone walls, and overhung with shivering tree limbs. A chill wind swirled dead leaves around their feet, and cut through Anna's sheepskin-lined jacket and denim jeans.

"Are you going to tell me what this is all about?" he asked. Anna kept walking. She was going to tell him about the arrest. She couldn't go through another night like last night. The memory of Emilio's flushed face watching her undress, tormented her. She banished the picture from her mind. Tomas didn't need to know about that.

"Why didn't you want me to let anyone know we're meeting?" Tomas said. He glanced at the empty path behind them. "If you wanted secrecy, then why meet at Cerro Santa Lucia?"

"It's close to your office," she said. "And I didn't want secrecy so much as privacy."

"Why privacy?" Tomas said. "Do you want to talk about Romo asking for a divorce?"

Anna took a deep breath. "No," she said. Her hands were cold inside the cashmere-lined gloves. "I want to find out why Romo was arrested."

Tomas said nothing.

"You're not surprised." She pulled him to a stop and faced him, the smog of Santiago forming a haze behind his dark head. "You've known all along, haven't you?"

"I had an idea."

"Why didn't you say something?" she cried.

"Why didn't you?" he countered. She was silent. "Was he arrested the day you told me he'd been sent on assignment?"

"The day before."

He glanced past her at an older couple strolling down the path toward them. "Come on, let's keep going." He drew her along with him, nodding to the couple as they passed.

"Tomas, how did-"

"Careful," he said. "You don't want to be overheard." For a minute or two the only sound was the crunch of sand under their feet. Anna's heart felt lighter than it had since the arrest. Finally. Someone to talk to. Someone to trust. She pushed away the nagging worry that tapped at the edge of her consciousness and kept walking.

Tomas broke the silence. "Why didn't you tell me before?"

"They said if I talked they'd kill him." Anna came to a sudden halt. "You won't tell anyone, will you Tomas? Promise!"

Tomas pulled her back in step and they continued climbing. "Of course not. I promise."

Anna swallowed. "I didn't think you would," she said. "It's just that I'm scared for Romo. For all of us."

"They've threatened the boys?"

"Yes."

Tomas' cheek muscle twitched. "What about you?" he asked.

"I'm fine," she said. She steeled herself to keep her feelings in check. "But I need your help."

"What can I do?"

"Do you know anyone who might be able to find out where Romo is, how he's doing, anything?"

Tomas exhaled audibly and shook his head. "I don't know, Anna. I can try but I can't promise anything."

"I understand."

He patted her shoulder with a clumsy gesture, then looked at her. "Why did you suddenly decide to tell me today?"

"What?"

"I said why did you tell me today? Did something happen?"

The cold reached the pit of her stomach. She couldn't talk about Emilio.

"Why was Romo arrested?" she said abruptly. Tomas shrugged and Anna continued. "Emilio said Romo's writing was dangerous. I read everything he wrote, Tomas - there wasn't anything dangerous."

They reached the top of the hill and turned to look at the panorama of Santiago. Anna usually marveled at the scene. There were no high rises, because of the danger of earthquakes. The height of the buildings was strictly limited. Today she gave the view a perfunctory glance and turned back to Tomas.

"What was Emilio talking about?" she said.

"I don't know."

"Damn it, Tomas, Romo was arrested more than two weeks ago. I want to know why."

"I know you're upset-" he began.

"No, you don't know."

The park was still deserted, empty of tourists and vendors. Sure that no one could overhear, Anna let loose a torrent of words. "You don't know what it's like to have strangers force their way into your home." A picture flashed through her mind of the two men subduing Romo in the front hall. "You don't know what it's like to watch your husband's arrest. You don't know what it's like to wonder if your children will be tortured or murdered just because you want to find out what happened to their father. You don't know what it's like to find out someone you've trusted since you were a child is your worst enemy." Her voice broke. The litany stopped. Her last sentence echoed in Anna's mind, and she looked at Tomas in horror. *Oh no*, she thought, *what if Tomas is working with Emilio?*

Tomas frowned. "What is it Anna? What's wrong?"

I can't tell, she thought. *I can't tell who's my friend anymore.*

"Nothing-" She broke off the sentence and darted toward the downhill path. Tomas chased her.

He grabbed her arm. "Anna, what's going on?" She turned on him, fingernails poised to scratch his face. He jumped back. She could have laughed at his shocked expression if she hadn't been so terrified.

"You're involved too!" she blurted, sure that she had ruined everything.

"Involved in what?" Tomas asked. He kept a wary eye on her nails.

"Romo's arrest."

"What?" He stared blankly at her.

"You said you've known from the start."

"Sure," he said, "But that's because-"

"It all makes sense now. That's why you didn't say anything." A part of Anna marveled at how coolly she could discuss it. That part of her was exultant at figuring out Tomas' complicity and handling it so well. The other part of her wanted to push Tomas over the cliff-like side of the hill.

"Anna, you're wrong," he said. "You know me better than that." He took a step toward her and she backed away. He sighed. "Yes, I probably do know why Romo was arrested." She listened, prepared for an attempt to snow her.

"Romo was writing underground political articles, used by groups like Amnesty International. He wrote about people who disappeared. He wrote about their families. He wrote about what happened to them in prison."

It's not true, she thought. *It can't be true. He'd have told me.* "You're lying," she said. "I don't believe you."

Tomas ignored her interruption. "We smuggled his work out of the country. Sometimes it was published, sometimes it would be used when proof was needed of imprisonment and torture."

"I don't understand," Anna said.

"The international publicity puts pressure on the government, Amnesty International starts letter-writing campaigns, and sometimes it helps. About a month ago, Romo thought Emilio was getting suspicious."

Stiff with anger and shock, Anna stumbled to a nearby bench and sat down. "No," she said. "I don't understand what this has to do with anything." She shivered, not sure if it was the cold wind or the cold inside her.

Tomas sat beside her. He took his time lighting

a cigarette before he spoke. "The day before he was arrested, Romo told me he had uncovered an incredible story. He wouldn't tell me any more. The next day he was gone." Tomas turned to her. "Anna, the only thing he did tell me was that the story somehow involved Emilio. Is there anything in his papers like that?"

"No," said Anna. "No, I went through every paper in his office and there's nothing." Something clicked. She sat up straight. That's why Juanita was always in the study and on her computer. Emilio has her looking for that missing article.

"What is it, Anna?" Tomas said. "Are you all right?"

"That must be what he was talking about the day Romo was arrested."

"What do you mean?"

"He kept referring to Romo's writing causing problems, and about his last article," she said. "But he didn't even look at the files upstairs. I couldn't figure it out."

"He knew the article existed?"

"Yes," she said. "Tomas, how long had Romo been writing these stories?"

"Off and on, since he got back from your honeymoon."

She recoiled as if he'd struck her. "Fifteen years?" she said. "And he never told me?"

"It wasn't safe."

"Safe!" she cried. "You son of a bitch! You should have told me." Dull red crept up Tomas' neck. "You should have-"

"That's enough," he snapped. He stubbed out his cigarette and tossed it over his shoulder. "You want to know why Romo never told you what he was doing? Because you never believed any of it was happening. Even when you came back from your honeymoon, after the coup, you didn't see it. You weren't interested in anything outside your front door. You were happy in your own little world."

"How dare you?"

"If you'd cared enough to know your husband, you'd have known what he was doing."

"Cared-" Anna choked on her fury. She rose and stalked back along the sandy path, toward the steps leading to the Alameda entrance of the park.

Descending the stairs, her steps slowed. Why was she so angry with Tomas? He wasn't working with Emilio, thank God. But Romo lied to her. Anna felt leaden with anger and despair. Their whole marriage was a lie. Her husband had never trusted her. Never believed she'd understand. Why did he wait so long to ask for a divorce? Why did he marry her in the first place?

She automatically turned left outside the park, following the Alameda toward Catholic University. She brushed past street vendors and skirted the throng of students and tourists. If Romo had trusted her, they could have worked it out. Why hadn't he trusted her?

"Are we still friends?" Tomas' voice startled her and she stumbled. She caught herself and turned to find him keeping pace behind her.

"What are you doing?" she said. She didn't smile. She couldn't. She might have to trust him, but it would not be easy to forget that he'd conspired with

Romo to lie to her.

He tucked her arm in his and strolled down the street. "I'm sorry," he said in a low tone. "I didn't mean to upset you."

"It's all right," Anna replied. He waited, but she didn't know what else to say.

"Why don't we pool our information?" Tomas suggested. "Maybe that way we can figure out what's going on."

"I told you what happened. They came and arrested Romo."

"Who came?" Tomas said. "Was it the police? The army? The CNI?"

"The CNI?" Anna glanced up.

Tomas shook his head. "Yeah, CNI. Central Nacional de Informaciones. Don't tell me you haven't heard of it."

"Yes, I have," she replied defensively, "But I can't keep all those initials straight. Anyway, they were police."

"Did they show any kind of warrant or papers?"

Anna felt a flicker of hope at his persistent questions. "No," she said.

"Did they threaten you or hit you?"

Anna nodded. She felt Tomas' muscles tense up, and she patted his arm. "It wasn't that bad. When I tried to go to Romo the one guy pushed me aside, and they told me not to talk to anyone. That was it."

She met his questioning gaze but didn't elaborate. He finally asked, "They didn't hurt you?"

"No," she replied. She could feel her face flush

and looked away.

"It would help if you'd tell me everything, Anna." He spoke gently. "You wouldn't be the first woman-"

"If you're trying to ask, did they rape me, the answer is no." Damn, she thought. Here it comes. Anna clenched her jaw, and then forced herself to relax. "They didn't rape me, Tomas, because as it happens, I have a protector."

Tomas stopped in his tracks. A what?" Anna pulled him along.

"Yes, a protector. Isn't that nice?" Her voice was brittle with sarcasm. If only he'd drop it right there.

"What exactly do you mean by a protector?" he said.

"Oh come on, Tomas," she jeered. "Figure it out. I'm protected from being raped and beaten by the peons, so I can be saved for someone special."

"Emilio," he said in a dead voice.

"Got it in one!" she agreed. Tomas reached his arm around her shoulder. She shrugged it off and glared at him. "Don't ever do that again." At the look of shock on his face, she burst into a harsh laugh.

"Anna-"

"Don't, Tomas," she said. He moved to keep up with her quickening stride on the pavement. "The last thing I need right now is sympathy. It won't change anything. What I do need are answers. Find some answers and I'll be grateful."

He nodded. "Do you want me to try to talk with Emilio?"

Anna jerked him to a stop. "Are you crazy? If you so much as look cross-eyed at him or give him any reason to suspect that I talked to you, Romo is dead. Pablo and Luis too. You don't breathe one word of this, Tomas, do you understand?"

"Yes, of course," he said. She searched his eyes for a moment, and nodded, satisfied. She took his arm again and resumed walking. "Sorry," he muttered. "I know better." A picture of Emilio on top of her last night flashed through her mind. Her step faltered. She could feel Tomas' worried gaze. "Has he..hurt you?" he asked.

Anna ignored the question. They stopped at a curb, waiting for a red light to change. Tomas watched her, but she refused to acknowledge his concern. The light turned green, and they crossed the street. He seemed to be waiting for her to speak. Her throat tightened. She had thought she'd fall apart if anyone knew. Instead, the despair and humiliation and shame hardened inside her to a toughness and a rage foreign to her.

"What is it, Tomas?" She glared up at him. "Do you want a blow-by-blow description?" He compressed his lips and said nothing. His silence infuriated her. "Fine. I'll tell you all about it." Her pace increased and Tomas lengthened his stride to keep up with her.

"Emilio let me know I had him to thank for my safety. If I cooperated with him, my sons would be safe and Romo would stay alive. He took me out to dinner. To concerts. All I had to do was pretend to love him." Tomas tried to speak. "No, let me finish. Emilio is very kind. He provides a babysitter who plays computer games with my sons. He brings me flowers. Last night he decided we knew each other well enough. He sent the babysitter home. We went up to my bedroom."

She snorted at the tears rolling down Tomas' cheeks. "Don't cry for me, Tomas. I'm lucky. Emilio told me so. Instead of being raped by a dozen soldiers, I get to play the part of his mistress." She scowled at his anguished expression. "And I'm very good."

Anna stepped to the curb and waved a taxi over. She turned back. "If you want to help me Tomas, stop crying. I have no time for tears. Find out something about Romo." She stepped into the cab, closed the door, and rolled down the window. "Call me when you get something."

Chapter Ten

August 3, 1988

Anna surveyed the library reading room from her corner table. Sunlight filtered through dirty windows, shimmering over a teenage couple a few tables away. They were bent over a book, their heads close together. The librarian posted near the door typed endless forms. The hum and click of the typewriter were punctuated by the soft snores of an old man, sleeping in a vinyl chair in the shadows of the wall.

Anna's fingers perspired against the plastic cover of the book in front of her. Where was Tomas? And why had he insisted on meeting her here instead of in his office? He hadn't told her whether or not he'd been able to find out anything about Romo. He'd said she was to be at the library at eleven in the morning.

She was to find the red-bound copy of Gabriela Mistral's collected poems, sit down at the corner table in the reading room, and wait.

Anna glanced up at the clock on the wall. Eleven-ten. Tomas was late. She drummed her fingers on the book. If this was his idea of a joke, he was in trouble. The teenagers turned to stare at her and she stopped drumming her fingers. They giggled, got up and went into the stacks. She swallowed her impatience and rested her forehead on one hand.

The sound of shoes tapping on the marble floor brought Anna's head up with a jerk. A young priest crossed the room and entered the stacks. Trying not to stare, she admired the mestizo blend of Indian and Spanish in his appearance. Thick black hair framed his dark face and accentuated high cheekbones. He was more than handsome; his face had the purity and innocence of an ascetic. Where was Tomas?

A whiff of familiar aftershave tickled her nostrils and Anna smothered a cry when a hand grasped her shoulder. Tomas slid into the seat beside her.

"Where have you been?" she hissed. He shook his head and unfolded the newspaper in his hand. Behind its pages, he signaled to her to pick up her book. He glanced at the teenagers who had returned to their seats, but they were absorbed in their work and in each other.

"Sit here and read for a minute," he whispered. Anna's brows contracted in a frown when he folded his paper and got up. Her book was still on the table in front of her. Her frown deepened when he returned the newspaper to a nearby shelf and stood browsing through magazines. What game was he playing now?

Without looking at her, he pointed to her book.

Anna snatched up her book. It fell open to a page marked with a folded sheet of yellow legal paper. She picked up the paper and looked at Tomas. He was leafing through a magazine with his back to her. She opened the paper and read.

You're going to meet someone who can help you. Don't look up from the book until I come back to the table. This is dangerous, so do as I tell you. Fold up the paper when you are done reading this, and lay it on the table, as if it's a bookmark.

Anna followed her instructions, eyes on the book. She sensed movement behind her. She pretended to read, turning pages that might have been covered with hieroglyphics for all the sense she could make of them.

The young priest brought his stack of books to her table, taking the seat opposite Anna. He would ruin everything. Should she tell him this place was already taken? Tomas had disappeared. Rifling through his books, the young priest spoke softly without looking at her.

"It's all right. Tomas is keeping an eye out for trouble." Anna forgot her instructions and stared at him.

A priest? She could still hear Padre Vincent in the confessional the day Romo had been arrested, his voice trembling, terrified of getting involved. Was Tomas crazy? What could a priest do except cause trouble?

"Keep reading," he reminded her, his voice scarcely audible. "Tomas said you needed help." She stared down at her book, resentment and hope warring inside her. When Anna didn't speak, the priest cast a swift glance at her. "Do you?"

"Do I what?"

"Need help?"

"Yes," Anna whispered. She turned another page.

"What's the problem?"

"Didn't Tomas tell you?"

"No," he said. "And we don't have much time."

Anna controlled her temper with an effort. "My husband was arrested. I can't find out where he is or if he's still alive." The need for reassurance after weeks of wondering was stronger than her resentment. She reached one hand across the table and pleaded, "Can you-"

She got a glimpse of snapping black eyes before he hissed, "Read!" She jerked her hand back as if she'd been burned, and bent over the poetry when another librarian wheeled a cartload of books into the room. Anna held her breath until the woman left.

"I might know someone who has information." The young priest continued as if there had been no interruption. "How do I know they can trust you?"

Anna's entire body stiffened. "How do *you* know-"

"It's a risk even talking to you," he said. "I won't endanger anyone else if I don't have to. Give me the details and I'll see what I can find out."

"Wait a minute!" Anna said. She looked around to be sure no one was paying any attention to them and kept her voice low. "How do I know I can trust you?" He shrugged. "Besides," she said, "If anyone finds out I'm asking questions, my husband could get killed."

"So could a lot of people," retorted the young priest. They glared at each other, ignoring their books. The priest was the first to remember their surroundings. He picked up two of his books and left her alone at the table.

Anna watched him in the stacks, keeping him in sight out of the corner of her eye. Why did Tomas have to pick a priest to help her? He'd probably turn out to be a coward, like Padre Vincent. She pretended to be absorbed in her book when he sat down again.

"I'll get in touch with you through Tomas if I think I can help," he said stiffly. He made quick, neat notes from the books in front of him while he spoke.

Priest or not, she needed him. "Dammit, you *have* to help me," said Anna. Her voice was raw with the suppressed fears of the past weeks, her eyes were bright with unshed tears, but he never looked up.

"I'll be in touch." He gathered his notes and books and was gone. She started to go after him, but Tomas had reappeared across the room and shook his head. She sank back down on the hard wooden chair. Tomas laid a finger to his lips and disappeared through the door.

Now what? She couldn't just sit there. But without Tomas and his priest, she couldn't make a move. If she did move without their help, Romo might end up dead. Damn Romo's stupid, quixotic need to be a hero. Why couldn't he be satisfied with his family?

Anna closed her book with a snap and snatched up the yellow paper. Her sneakers squeaked on the library floor as she walked out.

August 4, 1988

"I did it, Mama," shouted Pablo. He hopped out of the chair and flung the joystick over his head. Anna caught it out of the air and set it back on her desk with a smile.

"Take it easy, Pablo, you don't want to break the computer do you?"

"I won't," he said. "But I won!" He stopped celebrating to tug at her arm. "Now it's your turn."

Anna ruffled her young son's curly black hair. He beamed at her with a joyous expression that was a poignant reminder of his father. The lump in her throat made it difficult to speak, but she forced the words out. "Why don't you play another game and I'll watch," she suggested. He reclaimed the joystick, and she settled back in Romo's leather chair, inhaling the boyish smell of her son. Peanut butter, old sneakers, and a hint of soap. The computer screen blurred in front of her.

She hadn't written a word since Romo's arrest. All she cared about was getting him out. It had been two days since she'd met the priest, and not a word from Tomas. She responded automatically to Pablo's excited chatter while she pursued her own train of thought.

The priest hadn't even told her his name. Common sense said he was being cautious, but she was tired of caution and patience. She wanted answers, action, something to do.

"I won again Mama!" Pablo bounced on his chair. He turned to her with a pleading expression. "Can I have some cookies?"

"Two," she said. He hurtled out of the room. In

the sudden quiet, Anna couldn't sit still. She got up and wandered around the study, a short trip that ended at the window. The neighborhood was bustling with late afternoon activity. She could see a group of girls jumping rope on the porch next door. A soccer game was going on across the street and two boys rode their bikes around the corner. One of them turned in at her house. Luis was home.

Thank you, God, she murmured. Emilio's assurances regarding her sons' safety didn't comfort her. She never knew when he might change his mind and withdraw his protection. Fortunately she seemed to be able to keep him interested. She vomited after every encounter in her bedroom, but as long as she kept him happy, he kept them safe. She couldn't do it if it were just for her. She'd rather die.

The kitchen door slammed downstairs, and she could hear Luis and Pablo arguing as they raced through the house. She met them at the study door.

"Mama, Luis says I didn't win," said Pablo. He had a cookie in each hand, and came to an abrupt stop in front of her. "Tell him I did!"

"Yes, he did," she said to Luis. "Don't I get a kiss?"

"Sorry." Luis stepped over and kissed her cheek. "I didn't believe him. I thought Juanita was the only one who ever won that game." Anna stiffened at the babysitter's name. She caught Luis watching her and deliberately relaxed her body.

Pablo had finished his cookies, and tugged on Anna's arm. "Come on, Mama, it's your turn."

"Why don't you play for a while, Luis?" she said.

"You said you would," insisted Pablo. He held the joystick out to her. He was always so sure of himself. Just like Romo.

"All right," she agreed reluctantly, and sat down. The boys stood at either shoulder and watched her play. She got absorbed in the game as the little creatures battled their way around the screen. The boys cheered every time she scored. She could feel their warm breath on the back of her neck, hear them breathing faster as she racked up points.

The phone shrilled, shattering the mood. "I'll get it," said Luis.

"No." Anna reached past him to grab the phone on Romo's desk. "I'll get it. Hello?"

"You have to finish your game," Pablo said. He tried to force the joystick into her hands, and Anna shook her head and turned her back on him.

"I'm sorry, I didn't hear you," she said. "Who is it?" She slumped against the chair when she heard Tomas' voice. "Just a minute, please." She turned to her sons. Pablo and Luis stood, staring at her. She couldn't take the time to explain. "Boys, go do your homework till I'm off the phone."

"But Mama," Pablo protested.

"Just go," she said. "I'll call you when I'm through." She waited until the boys left reluctantly. She shut the door behind them, then spoke into the phone, "All right, Tomas, where have you been?"

"I'm fine thanks, how are you?" he said. She could almost see his mocking smile on the other end of the line.

"Don't play games with me," she snarled. "What's going on?"

100

There was a pause. "Can you meet me for lunch tomorrow? At McDonald's?"

"McDonald's? Tomas, is this some kind of a joke?"

"No," he said. "We need to talk about your progress since our last meeting. You know, your religious story?"

Anna realized he must be talking in some kind of code. Maybe he was afraid the phone was bugged. Religious story could mean the priest. "Yes," she said. "We do have some things to go over. What time?"

"See you at noon. Say hi to the boys." He hung up before she could say anything else. She listened to the dial tone for a moment before replacing the receiver. Was there really that much danger? It all seemed a little melodramatic. Then she thought about the consequences if Emilio found out what she was doing, and shuddered.

She looked at the game screen. Her little man was dead. Caught by one of the things chasing him. She snapped off the computer and went to find her sons and apologize.

Chapter Eleven

August 7, 1988

"There you are!" Anna rushed over to the window table in the crowded McDonald's. The priest from the library sat across from Tomas, a tray full of food between them. Tomas tried to speak through a mouth full of Big Mac, and choked.

"Who is your friend, Tomas?" the priest said. Anna gaped at him, wondering if he'd lost his mind. An urgent frown from Tomas clued her in. It was an act. Their caution struck her as excessive in that setting, but she played along.

Tomas cleared his throat and stood up. "Anna, this is my friend, Padre David. Padre, Anna is one of my favorite clients."

Padre David pointed to one of the empty seats. "Won't you join us, Anna?" he said.

"All right," she agreed. Before she could sit down, Tomas held up his sandwich. Anna sighed. "I'll go get my food and be right back."

She stalked over to the line. This was ridiculous. Who was going to see them? They were in McDonald's, not some underground hangout.

A middle-aged woman took her order. Anna counted and recounted her change while she waited. The meeting had better be worth it.

"Sorry to be so long," she said, when she got back to the table. Tomas ignored her sarcasm and drank deeply of his milkshake. Anna unwrapped the hamburger she didn't want and took a bite. The pungent flavor of onions, mustard, pickles and ketchup was overwhelming. She gulped it down, waiting for one of them to say something. After a few bites, she lost patience. "So what can you do to help me?" she asked, turning to Padre David.

He watched her juggle the messy sandwich. "Tomas, could you get me another cup of coffee?" he said. He flashed an apologetic smile at Tomas, who got up and went over to the counter. The smile disappeared when he turned back to Anna. "Are you trying to get him arrested?" he asked softly.

Anna almost swallowed an ice cube. "No," she gasped. "Why would you think that? Tomas is one of my best friends."

"You have a strange way of showing it." Padre David leaned closer. "Tomas has gone out on a limb to help you, and at the very least you could follow his lead. Try to look natural and keep your voice down."

"You're both so dramatic," Anna said. I'm sorry if I'm not behaving appropriately, but it's hard for me to take the James Bond routine seriously." Tomas brought three cups of coffee back to the table and sat down.

"Did you take your husband's arrest seriously?" Padre David said.

"Yes, of course," Anna said. "But that-"

"-was different." Padre David finished the sentence for her. She added sugar and cream to her coffee to hide her confusion. His next words came out slowly and deliberately. "Your lack of understanding is why I'm reluctant to pursue this any further."

Anna and Tomas stared at him. Tomas was the first to speak. "Padre David, I thought that's why you were willing to meet with Anna. To help her."

"I know you did," he said, his voice warm with affection. The warmth chilled abruptly when he challenged Anna. "Why should I help you?"

"Well, you'd really be helping my husband," she said.

"But I don't know your husband. Why should I endanger myself or anyone else for him?"

"You're a priest!" she said.

"So?"

"Dammit, you're supposed to help people." Annoyed as she was, Anna spoke in a low tone. A note of pleading crept into her voice, "Aren't we as much in need as anyone else? We're both good Catholics." Her desperation grew when he didn't respond.

"I'll pay you, if that's what you want."

"Anna!" Tomas protested. Padre David silenced him with a gesture. Anna was baffled. What did the man want her to do, jump through hoops? What would it take to convince him?

"What do you want me to say?" she demanded. His calm silence infuriated her. "Forget it. I'll take care of my own family."

She stood up and grabbed her tray. Her hand hit the cup and coffee flew all over the table. Neither man spoke while she threw napkins on the pool of liquid with shaking hands. She was sure everyone in the place was watching her. A strong, warm hand covered hers.

"Sit down," said Padre David. Anna sat. "Now maybe you understand a little of the desperation and the sense of danger felt by these people every day," he said. "We protect each other. Not only your husband's life-"

He stopped speaking abruptly. A hush fell over the restaurant, and Anna turned toward the entrance with everyone else. Four soldiers stood inside the door. One went over to speak quietly to the woman at the counter who'd served Anna. She pointed to the kitchen behind her, face red.

The soldier turned and motioned to his comrades. They disappeared into the back. Anna opened her mouth to ask what was going on, but Tomas shook his head. She noticed him exchange worried glances with Padre David, and felt butterflies in her stomach.

There were screams from the kitchen. Her heart pounded. The soldiers came out, dragging a man in his early twenties. He screamed, "Don't let them take me! Help me!" No one moved.

Anna gasped when he clutched the arm of a woman near the door and held tight. The woman tried to pull away. Why didn't someone help him? The soldiers pried the man's fingers off the woman's arm and pushed him toward the door.

I can't watch this, she thought. It's just like Romo. I have to do something. Before she could move, Tomas, as if reading her mind, had grasped her firmly by the upper arm and prevented her from moving. The soldiers dragged the man, screaming, outside and into a waiting van. Anna watched the van pull away, and then turned to Tomas.

People started talking, as if nothing had happened. The normal sounds of a busy fast-food restaurant resumed; the clink of money in the register, the murmur of conversation, the rustle of food being unwrapped.

"What's the matter with you, Tomas?" Anna's voice was unsteady. He met her glare with a stony expression.

"It wouldn't help Romo if you got arrested, too," he said.

"But-"

Padre David interrupted her protest. "I'll help you," he said.

Anna swiveled to face him. "You will?"

"I'll be in touch soon. See you later, Tomas." His exit was swift and Anna immediately lost sight of him in the teeming crowds outside the window.

She turned back to Tomas, her brow furrowed. "Wait a minute, I don't understand."

"Not now, Anna," he said. "Will you be okay if I

go back to the office?"

"I guess," she said. "I should get home anyway." He rose from the plastic seat with a grimace. "Can he really help us?" she asked.

"Yes, if anyone can," said Tomas. "Take care of yourself, Anna." He dropped a kiss on the top of her head and strode out the door.

Anna looked around. People were eating, talking, reading. She got up, threw out her trash, and left.

The crowd on the Alameda swept her along the sidewalk, headed in the direction of the car park where she had left her Land Rover. A hard, muscular arm snaked out of the crowd to link with hers. Anna jumped.

"Nice to see you again Anna," said Padre David, smiling down at her.

What was it with this priest? Why was he so paranoid he had to pretend they were just running into each other?

"Hello Padre, how are you?" she said. Anna tried to see if anyone was following them or watching. A nudge on the arm brought her attention back to the man beside her. He was chatting easily while they strolled along, arm in arm, but she felt the tense muscles in his forearm.

"-are you listening?" Padre David's sharp question penetrated her awareness.

"I'm sorry," she said. "What did you say?"

"I said that if you have time right now, there is someone I'd like you to meet."

"Do you mean-"

"Do you have a half an hour?" he said, interrupting her eager question.

"Yes. Where are we going?"

"Just keep talking and follow me," he said. He turned down the next block, heading toward the Parque O'Higgins. "Tell me how you met Tomas. He says he's known you since the University."

"Yes," she said. She hadn't meant to be curt, but she wanted to ask him why he had left her in McDonald's, only to accost her now. She responded to his conversational efforts, dimly aware of the direction they took. He steered them into a dingy yard on a quiet side street.

"Is this it?" she said. He nodded and placed a finger on his lips. He released Anna's arm and knocked firmly on the door. A girl of about twenty opened it at the second knock. She ushered them into a shabby living room.

"Hello Carmen. Is Bernardo home?" asked Padre David. The girl cast a scared look at Anna and said nothing. "It's all right, she's a friend." Carmen clasped her hands in front of her and chewed her lip. Anna wondered if they'd get to see this Bernardo, much less talk to him. Not if it was up to Carmen.

The wail of a baby pierced the stillness. A man not much older than Carmen appeared with the crying baby in his arms.

"Sorry, querida. She won't take the bottle-" he stopped when he saw them. "Carmen didn't tell me you were here."

"We just arrived," said Padre David. The man looked warily at Anna. "Anna, this is Carmen, Bernardo and their baby Stefano."

Anna acknowledged the introductions with a nod. Bernardo did the same. Under cover of handing over the baby, Bernardo pulled Carmen aside and spoke urgently to her. She argued, but then with a backward glance she took the crying baby and left.

"Please sit down," said Bernardo, gesturing to a white wicker couch with faded cushions and a matching chair. Anna sat on the lumpy couch with Padre David beside her. Bernardo hesitated, then sat on the edge of the chair. "What can I do for you, Padre?"

"Anna's husband is the man I mentioned this morning." Anna looked at Padre David in astonishment.

"She needs information," he said. "I told her I might be able to help."

Bernardo studied Anna while Padre David spoke. She did her best to ignore him, but she could feel her face flush.

"Are you sure we can trust her?" asked Bernardo. Anna struggled to push herself up from the sofa, but subsided under Padre David's restraining hand.

"You know I wouldn't have brought her here if I thought there were any danger," he said.

"Si," Bernardo conceded. He glanced at Anna again.

"I want to know what's happened to my husband," she said. "It's been weeks. Can't you tell me *anything*?" The distress in her voice seemed to touch Bernardo. He got up and went over to the window, peering out through tattered gauze curtains.

"I do know something about what goes on in the prisons," he said. "And who is in them." He stood at the window, his back to them. Anna waited impatiently for him to continue. When he remained silent, she decided to prompt him.

"*How* do you know?" she asked. He wheeled sharply and glared.

"Why do you ask that? Who are you? How do I know you didn't lie to the Padre?"

Anna reeled. She was dumbfounded by his reaction. Padre David interceded calmly, his voice deep and soothing.

"Bernardo, you know I would never put you and Carmen and the baby in any danger." Bernardo's eyes shifted to the priest. "Anna doesn't understand she shouldn't ask too many questions. She's never been involved in anything like this before."

The comforting monotone went on, and Bernardo visibly relaxed. Padre David stopped and looked at Anna. She knew he wanted her to say something.

"I'm sorry, Bernardo," she said. Trying not to alarm him again, she chose her words carefully. "I'm terrified for my husband and my two boys. You can understand that. I didn't mean to say the wrong thing. Please accept my apologies."

Bernardo surprised Anna by chuckling. "I knew you weren't a plant when I fired those questions at you," he said. "The look on your face was pretty revealing. You better develop a poker face if you're going to get involved in this business."

Padre David brought them back to the matter at hand. "Can you get any information for Anna?"

"What is the name of your husband?" he asked.
110

"Romo or Romulo Peregrino," she said. Hope flickered in her heart.

"When was he brought in?"

"Almost a month ago."

Bernardo said nothing. The flicker of hope inside her died.

"Can you let me know if you find out anything?" said Padre David. He and Anna got up to go. Bernardo stared at the floor. He lifted his head and looked directly at Anna.

"He's in the prison near the main army barracks."

Anna's knees buckled. She dropped back onto the couch. Padre David put a hand on her shoulder, but she shrugged him off and sat up straight.

"How is he? Is he all right? Did you see him?" she said. She faltered and stopped at Bernardo's sad smile.

"Señora, I told you all I know. He was brought into the prison the day he was arrested. Whether he is still there, or alive, I don't know. I'm sorry."

Anna buried her face in her hands. It was too much. To get information after weeks of waiting and worrying, only to realize that anything could have happened in the meantime. She raised her head and met Bernardo's concerned gaze.

"Thank you for your help." She got up and held out her hand. He shook it gravely. Her shoulders were straight and her head high when she and Padre David left the house.

"Are you all right?" he asked as they walked down the sidewalk.

Anna ignored the supporting arm he offered. "I'm fine. What's our next step?"

"You wait until Tomas gets in touch with you." He had to hurry to keep up with her. In boots and jeans she could move quickly. Quick movement felt like action.

"Do you have plans for this weekend?"

Anna looked at Padre David blankly, then realized he was trying to make it look as if they were carrying on a normal conversation.

"Yes," she said. "I'm going skiing."

"It's been years since I've been on skis. I'm sure you'll have a wonderful time."

"Yes, wonderful," Anna echoed in a hollow voice. Emilio was taking her to Portillo for the day. She was not looking forward to the skiing.

"I have to leave you here," said Padre David when they reached the entrance to a metro station. "Can you get back to your car?"

She looked at the street signs, feeling like she was waking up out of a bad dream. "Of course," she said. "When will I hear from you?"

"You won't."

Anna looked at him, eyes narrowed. Before she could object he went on. "I'll call Tomas and Tomas will call you. It's safer that way."

She nodded. He started down the subway stairs and turned to wave a casual goodbye.

"God bless you, Anna."

"Thank you Padre."

Chapter Twelve

August 13, 1988

Anna felt free for the first time in weeks. She hadn't expected to enjoy the skiing since it was with Emilio. But here she was, flying down the mountain on skis, the powder was deep, the run was deserted, and Emilio was far behind. Suddenly his dark figure swept past her, appearing out of nowhere in a daring maneuver. She slowed to a crawl, but Emilio pulled up a few meters down the hill and waited for her.

Portillo was the ski resort where her parents had vacationed for several weeks every year. Anna had been with them on most of those vacations, along with Emilio and his wife, Anita, until 1972, when an avalanche killed Anna's parents and Anita. Everywhere Anna turned at Portillo, she came face-to-face with her parents' ghosts. In her imagination she saw their dear faces, contorted with disgust because she was there as Emilio's mistress.

"You scared me, flying by that way," said Anna when she came to a halt beside Emilio. He preened at what he took to be a compliment.

"Are you ready for the last part?" he asked, surveying the rest of the mountain. His athletic body was vibrant with tightly leashed energy. Anna shuddered inwardly at what that might mean on the drive home. She had been able to hold him off on the trip to Portillo by chattering about the weather, the skiing, and his prowess in years past.

What she really wanted to do was ask him about the prison Bernardo said Romo was in. Emilio had said not to mention Romo's name again in public, but there weren't any eavesdroppers on the side of the mountain.

"Could we sit down for just a minute so I can catch my breath?" asked Anna. "I'm not in quite the shape you are."

"I think your shape is just fine, my dear," Emilio purred. "I wouldn't change a thing."

Anna turned away; afraid Emilio would see the revulsion in her face. She pretended to look for a place to sit. He skied over to a nearby log, and she glided behind him. He didn't sit next to her, but stood and admired the snow-covered Andes as if they were one of his investments that had paid off handsomely.

They were on the most difficult slope of the day, but Anna wasn't as winded as she'd implied. She needed a chance to talk to him. Emilio shifted impatiently on his skis. It was now or never.

"Emilio would you mind if I ask you something?" she said. His eyes narrowed. She wondered if he already knew what she was going to ask.

"What?"

"I just wondered, I know you said not to speak of Romo again in public, but we're alone here. Could you tell me if he's all right, if he's still in the same prison?" Her disjointed rush of words was arrested by the black scowl that darkened Emilio's face. Anna watched him, breathless.

"You aren't to mention his name to me again, is that clear?"

Anna was stunned by his terse words. What did he mean? Was Romo already dead? She persisted. "But why? What about the article you want? Maybe I could-"

"That's enough!" he thundered. "Do you want those sons of yours to be there when we get back?" Anna quailed.

"I'm sorry Emilio," she said. "I didn't understand. I thought you meant in public." She knew she was babbling, but she had to find the right words to calm him down. "I won't say anything again. I just thought maybe I could help. I'm sorry." His frown lightened. The cynical side of her said, *you've got him honey. A little begging goes a long way, and a little seduction even further.*

She brought forth her sauciest smile and taunted him, "Bet you can't catch me!" She went into a tuck position from her seat on the log, and swooped past him. She could hear his shout of laughter behind her, and the knot of fear in her stomach began to untie

115

itself. As long as she could sidetrack him, her sons should be safe.

He caught up with her halfway to the bottom, and started a game she'd often seen him play with his wife. He'd made up a variation of the cueca, the Chilean courting dance, on skis, in which he was the ardent lover, and she was his sweetheart. He showed off for her, matched his speed to hers, and at the bottom, caught her in his arms and kissed her.

The men working at the chalet pretended to ignore them, but Anna noticed their sly glances and knowing grins. She burned with shame, but held her head high. It was a small price to pay. Her sons would live another day.

Inside the chalet, Emilio stretched his legs in front of the roaring fireplace, a brandy snifter in his hand. His eyes devoured Anna. She tried not to notice, tried to keep up a one-sided conversation. She drank very little of the brandy, sure that she'd need a clear head for the drive home. There would be no chance she could hold him off completely, but a clear head would help her control what happened, and how far it went.

Drawn by the intensity of his gaze, she looked at Emilio. Sitting there in his scarlet and navy sweater and navy slacks, his silver hair immaculate and face tanned from the wind, he looked like the friend of her childhood. It was only when she let herself meet his eyes that she could see the difference.

"Do you like what you see?" His deep voice startled her, and she turned to the fire as if to hide a blush. It was difficult to disguise her contempt for him.

She murmured into her glass, "Wouldn't any woman?" He growled with satisfaction, and she

116

decided to prime him for the trip home. "Don't be so modest, Emilio," she said in her most provocative voice, still facing the fire. "You know all the women here are jealous of me."

There was the crash of breaking glass. Anna turned, startled. Emilio's brandy snifter lay shattered on the stone fireplace.

"I think it's time we started back," he said. He pulled Anna to her feet and thrust a handful of bills at the waiter.

The Rolls waited in front of the chalet, its motor running. Anna climbed in under Emilio's passionate gaze. Snow crunched under the tires as they began the long drive back to Santiago. Anna noticed the chauffeur's obvious interest in the rear-view mirror. She reached over and hit the button that would roll up the window between the front and back seats, and give them privacy. Emilio might not care, but she was damned if she'd perform for an audience.

She smiled at Emilio, her stomach tied in knots. He smirked back at her. She steeled herself, knowing she had to make a move before he did.

"We don't need him, do we?" she asked.

"Whatever you want," replied Emilio. She could see the pulse beating at the base of his throat, and she knew she had him.

"Whatever I want?" she repeated quizzically. He nodded. "Then take off your sweater." He pulled the sweater over his head. His skin had a slight sheen of perspiration from the warmth of the fire in the chalet.

She raked his chest with her nails, and noted with satisfaction his rapid breathing. As much as possible she avoided kissing his mouth. That wasn't too

117

difficult as long as she was willing to use that mouth to good effect elsewhere.

"Turn around," she said. He obeyed instantly. Anna began alternating rhythms. First massage his shoulders, neck and back. Then rain soft, wet kisses on his neck and shoulders while her nails raked his back, sides, and arms. His groans of pleasure were her barometer.

"Lie down," she said. He lay back on the seat, while she knelt beside him on the plush carpeting. She massaged his chest and stomach, while her tongue darted along his neck. Her mouth worked its way slowly from side to side, traveling down to his armpits, sucking, and working its way back. He writhed under her hands and mouth, and tried to pull her on top of him. She eluded his grasp and unzipped his pants. She tongued his navel while both hands disappeared inside his pants. Seconds later, it was over.

Anna breathed a silent sigh of relief and stole a surreptitious look at her watch. With any luck, he might fall asleep for the rest of the trip home.

Emilio opened his eyes. He glowed with satisfied lust. Her heart sank when his hands swiftly pulled her on top of him.

Chapter Thirteen

August 30, 1988

"Thanks for coming on such short notice." Padre David spoke quietly at the entrance to the metro station.

"Where are we going?" said Anna. Her eyebrows rose when he steered her toward the southbound line.

"There's a woman I want you to meet. She lives in one of the tenement areas beyond the last stop." Padre David took a few steps away from Anna and pretended to be absorbed in the advertisements on the wall. This time his caution didn't surprise her. A quick survey of the platform confirmed her feeling that no one was watching them. At the rumble of the approaching train, Padre David walked past her and said, "Watch me, and when I get off, follow."

The squeal of the brakes drowned out any further communication. Padre David boarded the train and sat under a colorful map of the metro system. Anna let a few people get on ahead of her, then took a seat across the aisle and a few seats down from him. She opened the book she brought with her, a copy of Charles Dickens' LIFE AND ADVENTURES OF NICHOLAS NICKLEBY.

Anna had read it before, but today it was for show. She glanced down and recognized the section in front of her. The book had fallen open to the chapter in which Nicholas rescues Smike from a beating, and they both run away from Dotheboys Hall. *You are my home*, she read, and her lips trembled. Those were the same words she'd once quoted to Romo before they got married. He'd been worried about her spending the rest of her life in a foreign country, and she reassured him with Smike's words.

A cough brought her back to the present. She looked up to find Padre David praying, his fingers moving from bead to bead on the black rosary. After what seemed like innumerable stops, he put the rosary away and got to his feet. Anna faked a yawn and closed her book. She exited the train behind Padre David. No one showed any interest in either of them. Once they reached the street, he took her arm.

"It's not safe for you to walk alone here, and I don't think anyone followed us."

The further they walked, the more Anna was shocked at the evidence of poverty. They reached an area where there were few real buildings. Most of the structures were little more than shacks or tents. The entire area was strewn with trash and smelled of refuse.

"Who are we going to see?" Anna said. There had been no time for questions when Tomas called that morning. She had been relieved to hear from Padre David. Weeks had passed since their last meeting, and she had chafed at the wait.

"Her name is Angelica," he said. "Her husband died in prison. She was tortured, then released. They had a baby. I'm not sure what happened to it." His voice roughened and he stopped talking. Anna didn't press him for any more details. They were walking through a section of the tenements in which about a dozen children of various ages sat on the cold ground outside. All of them, from the smallest toddlers to the school age youngsters, watched Anna and Padre David with a listless demeanor.

Anna thought back in wonder to the time before Romo's arrest. How was it possible she had lived in Santiago for all these years and never seen what she was seeing now? Why hadn't she believed Romo when he told her about the urban shantytowns and the despair in them? Anna knew she hadn't wanted to believe. She had had a happy little life with her sons and her husband, and she hadn't wanted anything to interfere with that. Shame swept through her in a sickening wave of heat.

She navigated a rutted path that had a few rough boards thrown down for a sidewalk. Padre David led the way into one of the larger shacks. She peered through the dim light. There was smoke coming from a fire in the corner, which provided the only heat in the place. It was a one-room shack with a corrugated tin roof and a wooden door grafted onto one of its walls.

The floors were hard-packed dirt, and the room held a rough wooden table, two wooden chairs, a cot along the far wall, and a few shelves nailed together. A woman was lying on the cot, one arm covering her face.

"Angelica?" inquired Padre David.

"Si." The woman lifted her arm slightly and looked at them. Anna stifled a gasp. This girl was too young to be married and a mother. In spite of her drawn features, Anna was certain the girl couldn't be more than seventeen.

"I'm Padre David," he said."We met last week." The girl stared dully at him. "I brought someone to talk to you. Anna, this is Angelica." Anna started toward the cot to greet her, but stopped when the woman shrank back.

"Thanks for letting me come," Anna said.

Angelica struggled up and leaned against the wall. "Sit down." She gestured toward the wooden chairs. Anna tried not to think about what might be crawling under the chair, and sat down.

"I understand you were in prison," Anna began.

"Si."

Anna was somewhat daunted by the monosyllabic answer. Padre David nodded encouragement to her.

"Padre David thought you might be able to tell me something about my husband. He was put in the same prison about six weeks ago."

Anna waited hopefully, but Angelica didn't respond, except to ask, "Do you have a cigarette?" Her hands plucked at the dirty blue blanket on the bed.

"Sorry, no," Anna said. Angelica felt the blanket

and pulled a crumpled pack of cigarettes from underneath. Anna noticed a box of matches on the table, and took them over. Angelica accepted them without comment, and stared at Anna's engagement and wedding rings.

"Nice rings," Angelica said. Anna smiled uncertainly and sat back down.

"Angelica, did you or your husband see Romo Peregrino in prison?" Padre David asked.

Angelica lit up with shaking hands and took a long drag. "Do you know why we were put in prison?" Anna and Padre David shook their heads. "We went to a soccer game at the stadium. When the guy at the gate tried to keep us out, my husband got mad. We had the money to pay. He didn't like how we looked, so he didn't want to let us in to mix with your friends." Her cold stare sliced through Anna.

"They put you in jail for that?" Anna said.

"We didn't do anything," Angelica insisted. "They wanted to know who we were working for and how we were going to arrange the assassination." Her bewilderment was evident in her voice and expression. Anna and Padre David exchanged startled glances.

There had been a big flap a few months ago when some plot to assassinate Pinochet was uncovered. Supposedly there were people in every strata of society involved. This woman and her husband had innocently been caught in the crossfire by being in the wrong place at the wrong time.

"Have you always lived here?" Anna said. She wanted to try to sidetrack the anger and self-pity and get her talking.

"Are you kidding?" Angelica snorted and puffed

on the cigarette. She flicked ashes over the side of the cot and spoke bitterly. "Would anyone stay here if they didn't have to? We came here from Antofagasta so my husband could find work."

"But couldn't you find somewhere else to live?" asked Anna.

Padre David jumped in. "It's difficult, Anna. People move here from the country, but there's no decent housing available. They put up buildings and tents and it becomes a community. If they're lucky, eventually the government gives them running water and electricity, but until then, they do without."

"And the more fools like us who come here, expecting work and housing, the worse it gets," Angelica said. "So I'm taking my baby and going back up north."

"When will you go?" Anna said.

"Tomorrow or the day after."

"Before you go, is there anything you can tell me about my husband?" Angelica looked at her shrewdly.

"What's it worth to you?"

"What do you mean?" Anna said.

"Will you give me one of those rings if I tell you what I know?" Anna stared at her, then down at her left hand. Her wedding band was a simple gold band with an inscription from Romo. The engagement ring wasn't flashy, but it did have a small diamond. She pulled off the engagement ring and Padre David protested.

"Wait a minute! Angelica, why would you ask Anna for her ring?" he said.

"Don't be stupid, Padre. I need money for the

baby, so we can go home." She looked ashamed for a second, and then shrugged her shoulders. "Besides, my neighbor took care of her while I was in prison. I have to give her something."

Anna handed her the ring. Angelica looked up at her with a strange expression. "I wouldn't do this for me, you know."

"I know," Anna said. "I have two children myself."

"Your husband was brought in the day I was released. I saw him being dragged in. I almost didn't recognize him because of the cuts and bruises, but Padre David showed me his picture. It was him."

"Cuts and bruises!" Anna said. "He had only been hit once or twice when they arrested him."

"Sounds like he put up a fight somewhere," Angelica observed.

"We should go now, Anna," Padre David said.

"But I wanted to ask-"

"That's all I know," Angelica said, her face hard again.

"Let's go Anna," Padre David said. "God bless you, Angelica, and good luck."

"Sure, Padre," she said. "But I need the luck more than the blessing."

Anna looked back when she went out the door. She could see Angelica through a haze of smoke, sitting on the cot, taking a drag of the cigarette, and appraising the diamond ring with narrowed eyes.

Chapter Fourteen

September 3, 1988

"Come on men, I'll race you!" Emilio challenged. He, Luis and Pablo spurred their horses ahead of Anna toward the corral. The boys hadn't done much riding. She held her breath until they pulled up safely in front of Emilio's top huaso, who took the reins of the three horses and led them to the barn. Emilio waited while she trotted up at a more sedate pace.

"You didn't race with us, Mama," Pablo said.

"No, ladies don't race," Emilio said. "And your mother is always a lady." She was afraid the boys might notice the warmth in his voice, but they were more interested in arguing over who had won their race.

While they argued, Emilio reached up to help her. She could dismount on her own, but was afraid to shake off the possessive hands round her waist.

He released her as soon as she hit the ground and took the reins of her horse. "Why don't you take your mother's horse in the barn and then we'll see if Serafina can scare up something to eat and drink." Pablo and Luis were thrilled to be trusted with the horse, thrilled to do whatever Emilio suggested. They led the horse into the barn, and Anna and Emilio started up the hill to the house.

It had been a difficult day for Anna. Emilio had insisted she bring the boys with them to visit his ranch outside Valparaiso. They were eager to ride again, and Emilio had promised them a fiesta.

"Thank you for giving them a wonderful time," she said. "I don't think they've had this much fun in quite a while." Emilio took Anna's arm. She disguised a shudder with a vigorous wave to the boys to join them.

Emilio's house was an old adobe hacienda, charming in its age, but efficient in all its modern conveniences. Things like the most up to date refrigerator sat on terracotta tiles that had cooled the kitchen for over a hundred years. He had shown her over the house when they first arrived. The boys had made it no further than the pool table, but Emilio wanted Anna to take the entire tour. She had wondered whether he was showing the house to her, or showing her off to his household.

Pablo and Luis were already ensconced in chairs on the flagstone patio, eating fried empanadas with chicken and drinking sodas. Serafina, Emilio's elderly housekeeper, was setting cocktails on the glass-topped table next to a tray of caviar.

"That will be all, Serafina, thank you," Emilio said. She nodded and left silently. "Please sit down Anna." He held the chair for her, and then seated himself.

"When is the fiesta?" Pablo said.

Luis frowned at his brother. "Don't be rude."

"It's all right Luis." Emilio was amused and turned his attention to the youngest Peregrino. "Are you in a hurry, Pablo?"

"No," he said, "I just don't want to miss anything."

"Don't worry. They won't start without us." With that assurance, Pablo was satisfied. He returned to his plate with renewed vigor.

"Will there be singing and dancing at the fiesta?" Luis asked shyly.

"Of course!" Emilio said. "What kind of fiesta would it be, otherwise?" In a teasing voice he inquired, "Don't tell me you want to dance with the girls already, Luis?" Luis flushed and didn't answer. Anna diverted Emilio's attention with a question about his estates. She kept him talking while the boys finished their treats.

The sound of strumming guitars drifted up to the terrace from a building beside the barn. Pablo threw a pleading look at his mother, but said nothing.

Emilio chuckled and said, "Are you ready to go down?" Before he could finish the question Pablo leapt from his chair and was halfway down the path to the barn. "Shall we go?" Emilio asked Anna. Both he and Luis offered her an arm.

Beneath his careless expression, Anna knew

Luis hid the fragile ego of a twelve-year old boy, trying to be a man. She didn't want to hurt him. Emilio waited, obviously amused by Luis' gallantry. Anna knew he wouldn't be amused if she took Luis' arm instead of his, since he was quite capable of being jealous of a young boy. She took both arms, and went down the hill flanked by her son and the man who saw himself as her lover.

Next to the barn was another building where the fiesta was to be held. It wasn't the right season for fiestas, usually held after the roundup. Anna knew Emilio had arranged this one for the benefit of her sons. He meant to impress her with his generosity, but she found his gestures oppressive rather than impressive.

People from all over the estate gathered in the barn, dressed in their most colorful clothes. Anna noticed the covert stares directed at the four of them. She burned with shame at what these people must think of her. Did they believe she was a willing mistress? Or did they know Emilio, and know that he had arranged her cooperation just as he arranged everything?

As the light faded outside, the strumming guitars and flickering lights beckoned inside. The building was transformed from an everyday ranch shed into a gaily decorated, noisy hall. There were huge wooden tables covered with food and drink at the far end. Pablo joined a group of boys his own age and disappeared into the crowd. Anna started to go after him but Emilio restrained her and said, "He'll be fine. The women will keep an eye on them." He guided her to a spot where they could lean against the weathered posts and watch.

After getting permission from his mother, Luis

joined two boys who were hanging around the musicians. Anna watched with pride as Luis picked up a guitar that was offered and played along with the men. He had only been playing for about a year. Romo had rarely had the time to give him lessons.

She could feel Emilio's possessive presence at her shoulder. There was no way to move away from him without offending, and she knew he would do nothing overt in front of a crowd.

"Would you like something to eat?" Emilio said. Anna wasn't hungry, but said yes anyway. It was a relief to be free of him, even if only for a few minutes. She looked around for Pablo. He was playing keep away with the boys at the opposite corner. His laughter rang out over all the other voices. He had had such a wonderful day. So had Luis. As long as she could keep playing along with Emilio, they would be fine.

Fury boiled up in her when she thought about how much they liked and admired Emilio. And after a day like today, he would be even more of a hero in their eyes. There was nothing she could do about that, and it was safer to leave it alone. Emilio could never replace Romo in their affections, no matter how much he gave them.

"I brought a little bit of everything."

Anna jumped. Emilio had a plate heaped with food, and a goblet of wine. "We can share," he said with an ardent look.

"The boys seem to be enjoying themselves," she said. "Your people have made them feel at home."

"They are at home," Emilio said. Her heart stopped at his words. She couldn't tell if that was a threat, or he was being polite. "Please, eat Anna," he said. She took a piece of chicken from the plate and nibbled. "Would you like to sit down?" he offered.

"No, thank you," she said. "After that ride it feels good to be on my feet."

He took a mouthful of wine, and then offered the glass to her. She shook her head. The last thing she needed was to be drinking, and out of his glass.

Emilio set the goblet on the ledge behind him and took a sandwich from the plate. He wolfed it down, watching the proceedings with paternalistic pride. Shy greetings offered to him were met with a genial nod, his chest swelling in self-congratulation.

"It's about time for the dancing," he said. Luis had returned the guitar to the musicians who had finished their practice and were now playing in earnest. Men and women gathered in the center of the barn to whirl to the lively music.

Anna's eyes blurred at the kaleidoscope of color. Most of the dancers were wearing elaborate traditional costumes that Emilio must have paid for. It was garish, but effective. The joyous mood almost carried her along with it. Then Emilio's arm would press against hers, or she would get a whiff of his sandalwood scent. The illusion would fade and she was back with a man she hated, in a place he owned, watching a display he had created for her.

"I should probably be taking the boys home," Anna said. "It's getting late and it's been a long day for all of us."

"Not yet," Emilio said. "They're just starting the cueca now. You can't miss this!" His eyes met hers in a command, not a request, and she turned to watch the dance.

A week ago he'd played at this dance on skis. Now, on the barn floor it was being performed with grace and sensitivity by a handsome young couple. Their imitation of the courting ritual, accompanied by the cheers and encouragement of the crowd, was both playful and touching. It was a dance that could be vulgar and obscene, depending on the dancers and the crowd. This was an exquisite performance, and Anna was moved in spite of herself.

At the height of the crowd's excitement, Emilio pulled Anna back from the bright lights. Her stomach churned. He pulled a small package out of his shirt pocket and handed it to her.

"I noticed that your hand seemed especially bare this past week, my dear. I thought this might fill the void." Anna reluctantly took the package and opened it. She gasped. Inside was a single, brilliant fire opal ringed by tiny diamonds in a gold setting. It was beautiful, yet simple, and she knew it must have cost a fortune. She closed the box and tried to hand it back to him.

"I can't take it Emilio, it's too much!" His cool, strong hands closed hard over hers.

"Of course you'll take it, Anna," he said slowly. "It is a present. You cannot refuse a present." The words echoed in her head, a reminder of his words the day Romo was arrested. If I give you a present, you will accept it, he'd said.

"Allow me to put it on, my dear." She stood mute while he took out the ring and eased it on to the third finger of her left hand. It was a perfect fit.

"Thank you," Anna murmured. She caught a movement out of the corner of her eye. Luis was staring at her, wide-eyed. As soon as she saw him, he scowled fiercely and melted into the crowd. There was a roar of applause as the dance finished.

"I can take you home now, if you're tired," Emilio said. He gestured to one of the men behind the drink table. The man disappeared, and in less than a minute reappeared with Pablo and Luis in tow. Luis didn't look at Anna or Emilio. Fortunately Pablo was spilling over with enough excitement for both of them.

"Could you give me a ride on your shoulders Uncle Emilio?" Pablo begged.

"Pablo, you're too big for that," Anna said. With a chuckle, Emilio swung Pablo up on his shoulders, high above the crowd. They headed for the door, with Anna and Luis behind them.

"Luis, please don't let Emilio see that you're angry," she whispered. He ignored her. She grasped his arm. "Please, Luis, this is important! Emilio tried to make this a very special day for you and Pablo. Don't spoil it." He gave her a scornful look and pulled away. She watched his stiff gait as he followed the others. What could she say to him that he would understand? If Emilio saw his anger it might infuriate him. That would be more dangerous than letting her son be mad at her. She would have to keep him from being rude to Emilio on the drive home.

"All right, boys. It's been a long day. Upstairs and get ready for bed."

Emilio hadn't noticed Luis' sullen silence on the ride home, thanks in part to Pablo's excited chatter. Fortunately, Emilio had dropped them off and hadn't insisted on coming in. Pablo scrambled up the stairs with enough energy to attack another day. Anna turned off the outside light. When she turned to go upstairs she saw Luis disappearing in the direction of the kitchen. She closed her eyes.

She could hear Luis moving around in the kitchen. There was the clink of a soda bottle. No soda before bed was a firm rule. Luis had always obeyed in the past, but Anna knew this defiance had something to do with Emilio. She opened her eyes and went into the kitchen.

"Why aren't you upstairs?" she said. Luis stood at the open refrigerator, pouring soda into a glass. She could hear Pablo upstairs, trotting from bedroom to bathroom and back again. "Luis, I asked you a question." Luis put the bottle back in the refrigerator and closed the door. He stood, his back to her, drinking.

Anna felt an unreasonable anger flood through her. She stormed across the room and yanked his arm, spinning Luis around to face her. The glass flew out of his hand and splintered on the floor. The startled look on his face brought her back to reality and she let go.

"I'm sorry I scared you," she apologized. He bent down to pick up the broken glass. "No, don't worry, I'll clean it up." He straightened. "What's wrong?" she said. She was afraid to hear the answer, but she couldn't leave things as they were.

Feet pounded down the stairs and Pablo rushed in. "What happened?"

"Be careful," Anna said. "There's broken glass and you're in your bare feet."

"Wow," Pablo said. "What a mess!"

"Are you ready for bed?" she asked him. Luis picked up some of the glass. Anna almost ordered him to stop, then saw Pablo's interested look. One confused son was enough. "Come on, give me a kiss and get upstairs." Luis laid paper towels down to absorb the liquid. Pablo kissed Anna on the cheek, his lips still damp from washing his face.

"Night Mama. Night Luis."

"Goodnight Pablo," Anna said. He lingered, waiting for Luis to say goodnight. Luis threw the wet paper towels in the trash.

"Mama, Luis won't say goodnight." Anna gave Pablo another kiss and a gentle push.

"Don't worry about your brother. We'll both be up soon." Pablo's lower lip stuck out. "Goodnight," she said firmly. He stomped out of the kitchen. Luis wiped up the last of the stickiness with a damp towel and threw it away. Anna put a hand on his shoulder. He shrugged away from her and refused to look up.

"Luis, please talk to me." He stood in stubborn silence. "Didn't you have a good time today?" She began to get angry again. "Dammit, Luis, what's wrong with you?" His eyes flashed up at her with resentment.

"What's wrong with me?" he cried. "Why did you let him give you that ring? Why haven't we heard from Papa? What is Uncle Emilio doing coming over here and taking you out all the time?"

Anna's anger dissipated. She wanted to comfort him, but she balked at answering his questions. Her son's bewildered face twisted her heart, but there was no way she could burden him with the truth.

"Uncle Emilio is a friend of our family. You know that, Luis. He's been our friend since I was a little girl. He knew I lost a ring and got it back for me, that's

135

all."

"I don't believe you! You're lying!"

"Luis, listen-"

"No, I don't want to listen to you. All you'll do is lie. I'm going to bed." Luis fled the kitchen. Anna felt as if she'd been kicked in the stomach. Luis was her baby, her first child. He had never spoken to her like that before.

She couldn't tell him the truth. The humiliation of having her sons know she slept with Emilio was unthinkable. It didn't matter that she had no choice. Luis' bedroom door slammed.

Anna crept upstairs, unable to forget Luis' look of hurt and astonishment when she grabbed him. She had never touched one of her sons in anger before. In her room, she flung dirty clothes into the laundry basket against the wall, and put on Romo's old sweats. She'd slept in them every night since the first night with Emilio. She couldn't sleep in any of her nightgowns any more.

She looked at the bed in which she no longer slept, and saw herself doing things with Emilio, to Emilio, that she never would have imagined possible. Was she changing inside because of what she did with her body? Was that why she almost hit her son tonight?

Curled up on the floor, her parents' quilt pulled tight around her, the crucifix above the bedroom door caught her eye. She hadn't looked at it since that first night with Emilio. She hadn't said a prayer she believed in since Padre Vincent turned her out of the confessional. But tonight she needed something.

I don't want my son to hate me, she prayed. But I can't explain. It would be too dangerous, even if I thought he'd understand. And he's too young. I know he's twelve, but he's just a baby. He's just a baby. Her mind kept repeating it like a litany, but her eyes were dry.

Chapter Fifteen

September 7, 1988

The door opened. Anna was disconcerted by the face on the other side. Unlike the drawn and fear-ravaged faces of the other people she'd met through Padre David, this woman smiled a warm welcome. Her eyes, which were level with Anna's, were a dancing green, framed by a halo of taffy-colored hair.

"Come in," the woman urged. She shut the door behind them and gave Padre David a hug. "David, it's so good to see you."

"You too Gabriela," he said, beaming. This was the first time Anna had ever seen a genuine smile from Padre David. He turned to her.

"Anna, I'd like you to meet Gabriela." Padre David stepped back while the two women exchanged greetings. Anna liked her immediately, responding to Gabriela's warmth and friendliness.

"I appreciate you taking the time to meet with me," said Anna. The smell of coffee came from a tiny kitchen off the living room. The apartment was small, but homey and clean. There was a bathroom visible beyond the living room door, and she assumed, a bedroom beyond that.

"Can I offer you both some coffee?" said Gabriela. "I just made a fresh pot."

"None for me, thanks," said Padre David. "I have to get going. Tomas and I will be upstairs if you need us." He closed the front door behind him.

"How about you, Anna?" said Gabriela.

"I'd love a cup of coffee if you're having some," Anna replied. Gabriela nodded and went into the kitchen. Anna toured the living room, listening to the clatter of cups and saucers in the kitchen. The living room was a reasonable size for an apartment, but every available wall space was lined with bookshelves, which gave it a claustrophobic feel. Anna crouched down to read the titles on the lower shelves. The variety of books surprised her. Everything from psychology to biography to novels to children's stories with a few gardening books thrown in.

"Do you take cream or sugar?" Gabriela deftly cleared the coffee table and set the tray down without a wasted motion. She wore a full skirt with a peasant blouse on top, giving her the look of a little girl at a tea party.

"Black, thanks." Anna seated herself on the

couch across from Gabriela. "I hope you don't mind, I've been admiring your books." Gabriela handed her the cup.

"No, not at all." Gabriela poured cream into her own cup and stirred. For the first time, she looked serious. "David tells me your husband is in prison."

"David? Oh, Padre David, yes - he is," Anna stumbled. She tensed, unsure what to say.

"I'm sorry. Why did they arrest him?"

For the next fifteen minutes Anna poured out the story of Romo's arrest, her own search for papers that might have caused his arrest, and the frustrating tidbits of information she had gleaned so far.

"-and that's it," said Anna. "I don't know if he's still alive or still in the same prison. And I don't know what to say to my boys when they want to know when their Papa is coming home." Anna gulped her coffee.

Gabriela watched her, a thoughtful expression on her face. She leaned forward to set her cup on the table and looked down at the floor. "And what is it you're not telling me?" she said softly.

Anna sat very still. Did she mean Emilio? Or the marriage problems with Romo? Or what? Their eyes met, and Anna knew she could talk to her in a way that was impossible with Padre David and Tomas.

"There is more," said Anna. "But I don't know that it's relevant."

"Why don't you let me decide that," said Gabriela. When Anna hesitated she said, "Look Anna, you don't have to tell me anything more if you don't want to. But I'd like to help, and the more you can tell me, the better."

"All right," said Anna. She took a deep breath and plunged. She told her about Emilio and their relationship, Juanita, and her fears for her sons. Gabriela listened without saying a word. She stirred a bit at the mention of Juanita, but didn't say anything.

When Anna finished explaining Emilio, she stopped briefly, then found herself talking about her marriage and Romo's request for a divorce.

"I understand now why he felt so alienated from me," she said. "I was blind to anything I didn't want to see. Until his arrest."

"Where were you during the coup?" said Gabriela.

Anna smiled. "On our honeymoon. We were in Ireland, staying at a castle owned by friends of my parents. We didn't even hear about it until we got to the airport on the way home." Anna flushed at her ignorance. "Romo got involved as soon as we got back, though I didn't know it at the time. I didn't want to hear it."

Gabriela poured the last of the coffee into their cups. "You're involved now," she said. "If your husband is still in the same prison, I might be able to get a message to him."

The cup shook in Anna's hands, and she set it carefully in its saucer. "What did you say?"

Gabriela nodded. "If I can reach him, what would you like me to tell him?" Anna stared at her. Contact with Romo.

"Anna, it's all right," said Gabriela. She put her coffee down and reached across the coffee table. She took Anna's hands in hers. "I didn't mean to startle you," she said. "It's because I'm a doctor. I work in the prison one day a week. If your husband is there, I should be able to get a message to him."

A message. What would she say? That she was fine? But she wasn't. Did she tell him she was sleeping with Emilio to keep him alive? What if Emilio had already told him? Would he even care?

"Anna, are you all right?" Gabriela's voice recalled her. "Do you want to lie down?"

Anna shook her head. "No, I'm okay," she said. She got up from the couch. "Could I use your bathroom for a moment?" She managed a smile. "Too much coffee, I guess."

"Sure," said Gabriela. "Do you need any help?"

"No, I'll be fine." She went into the little bathroom and splashed cold water on her face. She was patting her face dry on a towel when she heard a thunderous knock at the front door. She dropped the towel. It sounded exactly like the day Romo was arrested. There was a cry from the living room and the sound of a harsh voice.

"Where did the priest go?" said the voice. Anna peeked through the crack of the bathroom door. She froze when she saw three soldiers surrounding Gabriela in the living room. She looked so small and defenseless next to them.

"We know he came here and left here less than an hour ago." The soldier speaking had his back to Anna. She could only see the breadth of his muscled shoulders and the threatening stance of his trained body. He appeared to be the leader, since he asked all the questions. "Where did he go from here?" he said.

"I have no idea," Gabriela said clearly. She was standing straight and tall, as if to face up to the soldiers. Although she never betrayed Anna's presence by so much as a glance or a twitch, Anna felt Gabriela broadcasting her thoughts. Don't move. Don't make a sound. Stay in the bathroom.

"All right," said the leader.

At that, one of the soldiers grabbed Gabriela's arms. The other one backhanded her across the face. Anna winced. A trickle of blood ran out of the corner of Gabriela's mouth, and her cheek was bright red where he'd hit her.

"Where is he?" the leader repeated.

"I don't know," she said.

The soldier backhanded her on the other side of the face. Anna bit her lip to hold back a cry. Gabriela closed her eyes and tried to lick the blood from her lip. The leader nodded again and the soldier punched her in the stomach. Anna flinched with every blow.

The leader circled Gabriela and the other two soldiers. Anna caught a glimpse of a hard, cruel face. It was the face of a man who enjoyed the job of hurting people. He stood again with his back to Anna, facing Gabriela. He reached out and fingered her hair.

"You really should cooperate," he said. His voice sounded calm, almost soothing. "We don't want to hurt you, we just want to talk to the good Padre. You know where he is - all you have to do is tell us!" On the last two words his voice rose, he grasped a handful of hair and yanked. Anna could see Gabriela's face, contorted with pain, and clenched her fists in sympathy. Maybe they would leave, now that it was obvious that Gabriela wasn't going to talk.

The leader shook his head. "You could make this so much easier." He stood contemplating her while he lit a cigarette. After a few puffs he nodded to the soldiers. "All right, go ahead." He sat down on the little couch and watched. The soldier holding Gabriela shifted his position so he could hold her with one arm. He used the other arm to lift her skirt and rip off her panties. The other soldier unzipped his pants. Without waiting to lay her on the ground the soldier rammed himself into her. Anna gagged. Gabriela was sandwiched between the two soldiers while one raped her. The one holding her kept a hand over her mouth.

The soldiers switched positions and stretched Gabriela on the carpet. Anna couldn't see her. She could only hear the grunts of the soldiers, the clink of their belt buckles, the thump of their bodies. She bit into the heel of her hand to keep from screaming. Sobs welled up inside her, but there were no tears. Every instinct in her shouted to help Gabriela. But she couldn't. There was nothing she could do. Finally they were finished. The soldiers zipped up their pants, smirking at each other. Anna watched, unable to turn away, sick with revulsion.

The leader got up. "Finished?" he said. At their grunts of assent, he motioned toward the door. He bent over Gabriela. "Please give the good Padre our message." He kicked her, stepped over her body, and left.

The instant the door closed Anna was out of the bathroom and on the floor at Gabriela's side. She tried to gently help her lie flat on her back, but stopped when Gabriela groaned. Anna went back into the bathroom for wet towels, and tried to wipe off some of the blood.

"I'm so sorry, I'm so sorry," she said. She bathed Gabriela's face with a damp cloth. Gabriela tried to move her arm, but cried out in pain. She tried

144

to speak, but had trouble forming the words. Anna was sure her jaw was broken. "Don't try to talk, Gabriela. I'll take care of you."

"Get out of here." The whisper was so faint and the words so garbled Anna wasn't sure she'd heard correctly. "Get out," Gabriela repeated.

"I can't leave you like this," Anna said.

"Get David," Gabriela whispered. "Please." Anna couldn't refuse the insistent plea.

"All right," Anna said. "But I'll be back." Gabriela closed her eyes. Anna stood up and looked at the broken body lying at her feet. She took the blanket off the back of the couch and lay it gently over her. "I'll be right back."

Racing up the stairs at the end of the hall, Anna fought back nausea. Padre David had said he'd be upstairs with Tomas. There was only one apartment on each floor, so she couldn't get it wrong. She banged on the door, chest heaving as she tried to catch her breath. The door opened a crack and a man she didn't know was looking at her.

"Is Padre David here?" she asked. She could see the man's doubt, and she couldn't blame him. She must look a mess; her hair in disarray and a desperate look on her tear-streaked face. "I need to see him. It's an emergency, please."

The door opened wider and she saw Padre David and Tomas. "It's all right, Francisco, we know her," Padre David said. He stepped past the other two. "Anna, what's wrong?"

"It's Gabriela. There were soldiers looking - for you. She refused to tell them where you were. She's - hurt." Anna couldn't bring herself to say more.

"Come on, Tomas."

The three of them ran downstairs and back into Gabriela's apartment. She was lying motionless on the floor. Both men knelt beside her. Tomas swore under his breath.

"Is she still alive?" Anna whispered.

"Yes," Tomas said. Padre David spoke softly to her for a moment, and then said something to Tomas that Anna couldn't hear. Tomas nodded and stood up. "Come on, Anna, I'm taking you home."

"No! We can't leave her now," she said.

"Padre David will take care of her. He'll get a doctor. It's too dangerous."

Anna was speechless. She wanted to escape this horror and get back to her home and children, but she didn't want to leave Gabriela.

"Anna," Gabriela croaked. Anna dropped to her knees beside her. She took Gabriela's hand, as Gabriela had taken hers earlier that afternoon. "Please go, Anna," she whispered. She coughed painfully. "Thank you, but please-" Her voice failed. Anna held Gabriela's hand to her cheek for a second, then let go.

She was grateful for the comfort of Tomas' arm as they left the apartment.

The trip home was a blur. Anna wanted to go back and help Gabriela, and at the same time she wanted to run home and lock the doors with the boys safe inside. She couldn't get the sounds of the soldiers' brutality, the sight of Gabriela's battered body, and the smell of the blood out of her mind. After what seemed like ages they were home, and Tomas closed Anna's front door behind him. "What time are the boys due back?" he said.

Anna looked at her watch. "Not for another hour." She hung her coat in the closet and turned to Tomas. "Do you want something to drink?"

"No thanks," he said. "Are you all right?"

"Not really." She sat on the steps, her legs unable to support her any longer, and faced him. "Tomas, what would you think if I did some additional writing?"

"You mean other than your children's books?" She nodded. "Like what?"

"I'd like to write about Gabriela," she said.

His brows contracted. "I don't think that's a good idea," he said.

"Why?"

Tomas rubbed one hand against his face and sighed. "It just isn't. It's a different kind of writing from what you're used to."

"Do you think I can't do it?" she said. Tomas' face seemed to close up. He folded his arms.

"I don't know," he said. "But I don't want to see you try."

"Why?"

"Why do you suddenly want to start with this?" he growled. "You're doing just fine with what you know, and you have a deadline to meet. Why would you want to take on more work?"

Anna took her time before she answered. Finally she said, "Because I was there today."

"So what? It was going on before you were

147

there. It will go on after you leave."

"Tomas, did you ever tell Romo not to write?"

"I-" He stopped and shoved his hands in his pockets.

"I didn't think so," she said. "That could have been me. I saw what could have happened to me - what might still happen. No one could write about it the way I could, because I was there."

"Is that the only reason you want to write about it?" Tomas challenged. "Wouldn't it be better to try to forget it?"

Anna shook her head. "Would Romo have done that? How can I? You were right Tomas, both of you. I didn't see what was going on around me because I didn't want to see. I can't pretend it isn't there any more, and I can't let it go on without trying to do something about it."

Tomas bowed his head and asked, "Will you just write about Gabriela, then go back to your book?"

"I don't know," she said.

His head came up and he glared at her. "I don't want you trying to pick up where Romo left off."

"Why not?"

"It's too dangerous," he snapped. Anna was puzzled by his agitation, but too tired to worry about it.

"The meetings Padre David arranges are dangerous too," she said. "You haven't said anything about that."

"No, because I thought that once you found out what you could about Romo, you'd stop there." Tomas took a deep breath and calmed himself. "If you start writing it will get more and more dangerous. Eventually you may end up in prison too. Or dead. Then what happens to Pablo and Luis?"

Anna buried her head in her arms. That was the one thing she didn't want to think about.

"Anna-"

She raised her head. "I love my sons. But I couldn't look them in the face if I didn't try to help Gabriela." She laced her fingers together and stood up on the bottom step so she was almost as tall as Tomas. "We're all responsible to try and make a difference. You and Romo always knew that. Now I do too."

Tomas' shoulders slumped. "All right, Anna," he said. "Let me know when you have something and I'll take a look at it. If I think it's okay, I'll get it to the right people."

She stood up and kissed him on the forehead. "Thanks Tomas. And thanks for being there today."

We're all responsible to try and make a difference. Anna almost laughed out loud when she remembered what she'd said to Tomas that afternoon. Brave words, when all you have to do is talk. How about when a little action is required? Like writing something.

She faced her blank computer screen, hands frozen on the keyboard. She had told Tomas she wanted to write about Gabriela. So why didn't she know what to say? Why wouldn't the words come? She could still see Gabriela lying on the apartment floor, and smell the sickly, sweet odor of her blood. She could still hear the moans Gabriela couldn't suppress. But Anna's mind and fingers refused to cooperate and translate those memories into words.

Emilio had said that the soldiers would torture her sons for the pleasure of hearing their screams. A picture flashed into her mind of Luis being raped by soldiers.

Padre David had told her once that the youngest ones, the babies, were the lucky ones. They could be sold to rich families to be brought up by people who wanted children and couldn't have any. Boys and girls of Pablo's age might end up roaming the streets, homeless, or they might be sold to someone whose sexual preferences ran to younger children. When the homeless children became a nuisance, the soldiers would round them up and shoot them, like so many vermin.

Boys and girls of Luis' age were rarely allowed to disappear into the streets. They were valuable merchandise. An unmarked, handsome boy of twelve like Luis would be worth a fortune in money or favors.

Anna pushed away from the computer. If she thought like that she'd go crazy. But she wondered if her sons would pay the price for her bravado.

A sound from one of the bedrooms alarmed her. She hurried down the hall to check on the boys. Luis was lying on his side, breathing evenly. His face looked peaceful in sleep, not like the angry, bewildered expression he'd been wearing since the fiesta.

Pablo was sprawled on his bed with covers rumpled and his pillow jammed against the headboard. Anna pulled the covers over him and lifted his head gently while she slipped the pillow underneath. His dark, curly hair lay in damp ringlets on his forehead. She smoothed his hair and closed the door behind her.

Back in front of the computer, her fingers flew on the keyboard. It might be a terrible risk to write about Gabriela. But the greater risk was not to write. She shut the distractions out of her mind, and kept typing.

Chapter Sixteen

September 14, 1988

     "I feel conspicuous here," Anna said, looking around the dingy bar. She sat in a corner booth next to Padre David, who was uncharacteristically dressed in torn jeans, a black sweatshirt with the sleeves cut off, and a denim jacket. He looked at home, slouched against the black vinyl cushion of the booth. Two men sat at the bar, both of them dressed like Padre David. Only one stool separated them, but each of them stared into his own drink.

     The bartender lounged behind the bar, reading the newspaper. He ignored the dirty glasses overflowing the sink, and only put down his paper to get a refill for one of his customers. Anna could see the grime worn into the linoleum floor, on a pattern that might once have been black and white. There were dirty glasses and plates on a few of the tables, and a crumpled paper napkin on one of the chairs.

The bar door opened and to Anna's overactive imagination the room seemed to shrink away from the bright sunlight streaming in. No one at the bar looked up at the short, fat man who entered. He was dressed in the same uniform as the others, jeans and sweatshirt. This must be the contact. He ignored them and shambled over to the bar. She swallowed her disappointment.

"Are you sure this was a good place to meet?" she asked Padre David. He nodded.

"Don't worry if you feel out of place," he said. "You're dressed like everybody else, and as long as you don't make a scene no one will pay any attention to you."

"Why would I make a scene?" she asked.

He took a swig of beer. "You never told me someone was looking for Romo's last article," he said.

Anna was surprised by the change of subject. "Why should I? And how do you know? Tomas?" She was unnerved by the grave expression on his face.

A shadow fell on the table. Anna's fingers tightened on her glass. The fat man sat down on the other side of the booth with a glass of beer.

"Anna, this is Rico," Padre David said. "His brother is in prison. Rico has been in touch with people from Amnesty International."

"I can't stay long," said Rico. His voice surprised Anna. It sounded far more refined than his clothes had led her to expect. He glanced at the bartender and the other customers. "I called Amnesty International because I wanted their help to get my brother out."

"Can they do that?" Anna said.

"Not exactly," he said. "They start letter writing campaigns for what they call prisoners of conscience. Only problem is, my brother hasn't been charged with anything, and the government claims they don't have him."

"So what happens?" she said.

"Without some kind of verifiable evidence that he's in prison, there's nothing they can do," Rico said.

"That's crazy!"

Rico drained his glass of beer, wiped his mouth with the back of his hand, and continued. "They have some people investigating my claim. The good Padre here thought you might want to try the letter routine. It's slow, but I hear it works. Do they admit that your husband was arrested?"

"I don't know," Anna said. "No one's said anything official. But I haven't been able to..." Her words trailed off.

"Anna's family has been threatened if she tries to find out what happened to her husband," Padre David said. "We're concerned that even an outside investigation might jeopardize her safety."

"*Who's* concerned?" Anna said. She wasn't aware that anyone had discussed outside investigations or Amnesty International.

Rico ignored her question. "I'm not waiting for their investigation," he said.

"Why not?" she said.

"Every day it takes them to investigate is one more day of torture for him," he said bluntly. "And it's often worst at the beginning."

"How do you know that?" asked Anna. Rico slid out of the booth with some difficulty, and went over to the bar. He came back with another beer and a bowl of nuts, and answered as if there had been no interruption.

"I was arrested last year myself. Fortunately they decided I wasn't important enough to keep. I was only in for a month, but it was enough." He pulled up the sleeves of his jacket and Anna saw with horror that his wrists still bore the scars of whatever they'd used to tie him down. "I want to get my brother out of there."

"What else can you do?" she said. He didn't answer her right away. She looked at Padre David but he shrugged his shoulders.

"I can prove he's in there," Rico said.

"How?" Both Anna and Padre David shot the word at Rico. In spite of their excitement, they kept their voices low.

Rico popped a handful of nuts in his mouth and washed them down with a gulp of beer. "A photograph," he said.

"A photograph of what?" Anna said.

"Of him. In prison."

"That's too dangerous," Padre David insisted. Rico clenched his jaw, but said nothing.

"I don't understand," said Anna, "How can you get a photograph of your brother if the government won't even admit he's in prison?"

"I can't tell you the details," Rico said. "But there is a way. It's risky, but I have to try."

Padre David shook his head. "Amnesty International would never set up that kind of dangerous operation. It doesn't make sense."

"They didn't set it up," said Rico. "Someone else did. Amnesty International needs authenticated information and documents, so that's what I'm going to get."

His florid face was serious, and Anna was impressed with his courage. She was also thrilled by the possibility of doing something that might get Romo out of prison. In spite of Padre David's reservations, it sounded like a great idea to her. Rico emptied his second glass and got up to leave.

"Wait, where can I get in touch with you?" Anna said.

"You can't. I'll tell my contact to get in touch with the good Padre here. Good luck."

"You too," she said. Padre David gave him an absentminded wave of the hand. Anna felt the tension in the arm and shoulder that were pressed against hers in the confines of the booth. "Have you heard about this before?" she said.

"No," he said, "It sounds dangerous."

"Would you ask Tomas what he knows about it and have him call me? You are meeting him later, right?"

"Yes, and yes." She started to get up, but he put a hand on her arm. "Anna, wait."

"What?"

"I have some news for you."

Panic fluttered in her stomach. "It's not Romo is it? Is it bad news?"

"No," he said. "No, I haven't heard anything about Romo."

"What, then?" she prodded. He turned and Anna was frightened by the profound sorrow in his eyes. "David, what is it?"

"It's Gabriela," he said. "Anna, I'm sorry. She died last night."

Anna felt a hard knot of grief and anger trying to force its way to the surface, and she fought to keep it buried somewhere inside.

"Thank you for telling me, David. I have to go now." She pulled away from his restraining hand and turned her back on him. She had to get out of there. She had to walk, to do something. He was saying something behind her, but she didn't listen. She escaped through the bar door and into the bright, winter sunshine.

Her legs moved of their own accord. Block after block, past the stores, past the hotels Anna walked. Automatically she obeyed traffic signals and kept out of the paths of cars and buses. When she turned at one corner, she knew where she was going. There was a small student chapel at the university that was rarely used. At one time it had been a place she could retreat when things overwhelmed her.

As Anna expected, the chapel was empty. It wasn't much more than a hut with stained glass windows, a little altar, a cross, and a few rows of chairs. Anna sat down in the last row of chairs. She felt a wail of grief and rage well up inside and bit her lips to keep it there.

Gabriela was dead. That beautiful, brilliant, generous woman - dead. The image of her body, bloody and beaten, had haunted Anna during the past week. In spite of her pain, Gabriela's eyes had been so alive. She had known that Anna didn't want to leave, would only leave if she told her to. So with every word an agony, Gabriela told her to leave.

With a shudder Anna gave in to the pain. Dry sobs wracked her. Her arms wrapped around her body in a vain attempt to contain her anguish.

Forehead resting against the chair in front of her, Anna realized dimly that not all of her grief was for Gabriela. Gabriela's rape, beating and death made it clear how fragile her own future was. Emilio's protection was a flimsy barrier that might be brushed aside at any moment. But for now it was all she had.

Anna looked up at the cross, her breathing ragged. The cross had always been a symbol of comfort and security for her while she and her parents moved from country to country. No matter where they went, there was always a church with a cross. The "house of God". And since God was our Father, it was her Father's house, and therefore, home. The only home she could ever count on.

Now that cross looked down on her from the bedroom wall when she was with Emilio. And it looked down on her here. And it gave her no answers. She was seeing Emilio again tonight, and she had no answers.

Without thinking, she spoke out loud. "What good are you if you let someone like Gabriela die that way? Why don't you find a way to help me? Why don't you care?"

158

"He does care, Anna."

Anna wheeled at the voice behind her. Padre David stood in the doorway.

"You scared me!" she said. She pretended to laugh at her fear, and then choked it back when the laughter threatened to become hysteria. "How did you know where I was?"

"I followed you from the bar." Padre David closed the door behind him and sat down across the aisle from Anna. "You were upset, and I was worried about you."

"Don't waste your worry on me," said Anna. "Or your prayers. That is, if you still pray."

"Yes, I do."

"How can you?" she cried. "How can you still believe in a loving God after what happened to Gabriela?"

"I don't know," was the unexpected reply. "Sometimes I ask myself the same questions."

"And what answers do you get?"

"That God's love had nothing to do with Gabriela's death," he said. Padre David met Anna's scowl without flinching. "We're given choices, Anna, from the time we're born. Those men chose to destroy a wonderful human being. That act had nothing to do with God."

"But how can you believe in a God that lets that go on?" she said.

"Take a look at the cross. Is what happened to Gabriela so different from what happened to him? *Men* did that, Anna, not God."

Anna looked at the cross, then looked at Padre David. She shrugged her shoulders. "I'm too tired to figure all this out. I wish I had your faith."

"Are you so sure you don't?" he said. "Why did you come here when you left the bar?"

"I don't know. I just started walking and this is where I ended up. It used to be one of my favorite places when I went to the University." He nodded. "You mean I came here because I was turning to God, however angry I might be?"

"You wouldn't be the first," said Padre David. "Often our heart leads us where our head would never think of going."

"I'll have to think about that one." Anna stood up and ran a hand through her hair. "It's time for me to get going if I'm to make it home before my sons." She opened the door and turned back. "Thanks, David, for following me."

"Mama, why are you going out again tonight?" said Pablo. He sat with his head propped on his hands and his elbows on the table. Anna recognized the signs of a sulk, an unusual mood for Pablo. She passed him a plate filled with seafood stew.

"I have to talk to Uncle Emilio, so we're going out for dinner." She dished out stew for Luis and handed it to him.

"But you go out with him all the time," said Pablo. "I want you to stay home."

Luis glanced at his little brother, then at his mother. He frowned and returned his attention to his plate.

"Eat your dinner, Pablo," she said. Her cup of coffee sat untouched.

At least Luis was speaking to her now, or he was when she spoke first. He rarely looked at her, and when he did it was with quick, furtive peeks. When he finished his dinner she said, "More?"

"No, thanks." He drained his glass of milk and watched Pablo shovel down the food. Pablo wore an unaccustomed frown on his cherubic face. His sulking didn't impair his appetite, and he finished quickly.

"What's for dessert, Mama?" he asked.

"Ice cream," she said. She cleared the table, scooped up two bowls of chocolate ice cream, and put them in front of Pablo and Luis. Both boys took their time eating. She checked the clock. Emilio was due any minute, and she wanted to finish up in the kitchen before he came. "Hurry up, boys," she said, "I have to finish getting ready."

"You're already dressed," Pablo said. He stopped eating to point at the black dress she wore under an apron.

"Come on, eat up," she said. "I want to get the dishes done before they get here." She was nervous about seeing Emilio tonight. Her feelings about Gabriela hovered close to the surface, and Emilio wasn't blind.

Luis finished his ice cream and carried the dish over to the sink. He started the water and poured in detergent without a word.

"Thanks, Luis," she said. "Come on, Pablo. Your ice cream will melt."

"I want chocolate sauce on it," he demanded. Anna shook her head and looked at the clock again.

"No, you've already eaten half, now finish it up." Pablo reluctantly took another spoonful. Anna stifled her irritation. Sometimes she thought Pablo was deliberately annoying.

Anna heard steps coming up the walk, then a rap on the kitchen door. She swore under her breath and went to answer it. Emilio didn't like to be kept waiting, but she didn't like to let Juanita touch anything in her kitchen.

"Good evening, Anna. Hello boys." Emilio's greetings were friendly. He didn't appear annoyed that she wasn't ready. Pablo grinned at him from over his ice cream, his sulks forgotten. Luis didn't turn away from the sink. "Luis," he said, "Your mother has you doing dishes! That's a woman's work, son."

Juanita entered quietly behind Emilio, laid her coat over a chair and went over to the sink. "Let me help you, Luis." She picked up a towel and started drying the dishes Luis had washed. Much as Anna didn't like her, she was grateful for the intervention.

"Are you ready?" asked Emilio. "Juanita can finish up in the kitchen." Juanita looked at him, her face unreadable. Emilio missed the look, but Anna noticed and was surprised. Who was the boss in that relationship?

"Let me get rid of this apron and kiss the boys," said Anna. Pablo gave her a forgiving smile after she kissed the top of his head. She went over to Luis, who barely turned so she could kiss his cheek. "I'll be back later. Be good."

"They'll be fine," said Juanita. "Have a good time."

"Two cups of espresso," Emilio said to the waiter. Anna watched him covertly, wondering what was wrong. He had been strange ever since they left the house - brooding, morose. No fear that he'd notice she was upset. She tried to keep up a flow of chatter, but he barely responded.

"Emilio." He appeared not to hear her. She laid a hand on one of his and he jumped. "I'm sorry," she said. "I didn't mean to startle you."

"You didn't," he said, though they both knew it was untrue. "I just didn't hear you. What did you say?"

"I asked if you've seen your friends Eduardo and Diego recently." If that didn't get a response from him, nothing would. She had been relieved when she discovered Emilio's jealousy kept them from socializing with his slimy cohort, Eduardo, but she'd have liked the chance to talk with Diego again.

Emilio shook his head. "Not really. Eduardo's been out of town. Diego-"

"Yes," Anna encouraged.

"Diego was in a serious automobile accident." A hint of a smile twisted his lips. "I'm sorry to say he didn't survive."

"Oh no," she said, shocked. *Was* it an accident? "I'm so sorry."

"Yes."

The espresso came. Anna sniffed the fragrant aroma and sipped.

"Anna, we need to talk a little business," said Emilio. He sat upright, alert and decisive, in contrast to his earlier abstraction.

"Business?" Anna's heart sank. Did he know

about Padre David and Tomas? Or Gabriela?

"Yes. I told you the day Romo was arrested that he was in trouble because of his writing. I want to see the article he was working on when he was arrested."

She stared at him. Not only was he talking about Romo, he was doing it in public. What was going on?

"You did see the article," she said, "You had a copy at the magazine."

"Not the one he wrote for my magazine," he said. "There was another article. It made reference to me. That is the one I want."

"I've never seen one like that-"

"You must have!" Emilio's fist crashed on the table. Anna stared at him, aware that every eye in the place was on them.

He must know about the underground article. What had Romo written that could upset Emilio like this?

"Is everything all right señor?" said the headwaiter, who had appeared beside the table.

"Fine. Leave us," said Emilio without looking up.

"Of course, señor." Anna had never seen Emilio lose control in public. His eyes bored into hers, as if he were trying to read her mind. I can't let him see that I know what he's talking about, she thought. It must be important to make him break his own rule and talk about Romo. She kept her expression blank.

"Perhaps you haven't seen it," Emilio conceded. His cold, handsome features resumed the urbane mask and he smiled. "Would you care to dance?"

"Thank you." Anna followed him to the dance floor, her mind seething. Juanita obviously hasn't found anything, or he wouldn't be this upset. Maybe I should look again. I have to tell David and Tomas.

Emilio took her in his arms and they swayed to the music.

Chapter Seventeen

September 20, 1988

"You said you wanted to talk before we meet them?" said Padre David. He was pacing on the sidewalk outside the Parque Ines de Suarez, bundled up in a wool jacket and scarf. Anna took his arm and they strolled down the path into the park.

"Yes," she said. "I want to talk some more about Rico's idea."

He glanced down at her. "Anna, I don't think you realize how dangerous that could be."

"I do, and I'm not sure I want to do it. I just want to know more about it." She fell silent at the approach of two elderly women. The women passed by,

166

absorbed in their conversation. "What did Tomas say when you told him?"

"What do you think?" he said with a grin. Anna rolled her eyes and Padre David continued. "He thinks it's a crazy idea." His expression sobered. "He's right this time. Tomas may be overly cautious where you're concerned, but he has reason."

"Why?"

"His other contacts aren't his clients. Getting you involved in the underground network is risky for him. And you're old friends. He worries about you."

"Too much," she said. Anna pulled her sheepskin-lined coat tight around her. "If I wanted to try getting photos of Romo in prison, could it be done?"

"I'm not sure," said Padre David. "Tomas does know something about it, but I'm not sure he'll tell me." He faltered.

Anna prompted him. "Come on, David, this is important. Don't clam up on me now." He guided her over to a bench beside the path. They sat. Padre David loosened and retied the scarf around his neck. Anna was baffled by his hesitation. It couldn't be a matter of trust. She knew he'd trusted her completely since the day with Gabriela.

"Tomas asked me not to talk to you about the photos," he said finally.

"Why not?"

Padre David shrugged. "He won't say. He just told me to please not discuss it with you, or encourage you in any way."

"But you are talking with me," said Anna.

"Yes."

Anna's entire body tensed. Whatever he was going to say, it was important.

Padre David was careful with his words, as if trying not to place too much emphasis on them. "I think you may be right," he said.

"About what?"

"That it could be worth the risk to get the photos," he said.

"You mean it?" she cried.

"Yes. All too often I've seen people who were unable to get help for loved ones in prison because there was no way to prove or verify the imprisonment. If you *can* get that proof, it might get Romo released."

"Will you help me?" she said.

"I'll try," he promised. "Let me see what else I can find out."

"By the way," she said. "When we met with Rico you said something about 'we decided an outside investigation was too dangerous for Anna'. Who is 'we'?

Padre David flung up his hands in mock surrender. "Guilty! It was Tomas and me, of course."

She wasn't amused by his attempt to placate her. "Nobody decides anything for me but me - do you understand?" she snapped.

He sobered. "Yes, Anna, and I'm sorry. But you haven't been completely honest with us either."

"What do you mean?" She bristled at the suggestion.

"You never told either of us that you thought Juanita, your babysitter, might be looking for Romo's article."

168

"Who told you that?"

"Gabriela," he said. Anna stared at him. "She thought it was important we know."

Anna slumped on the bench, a sudden wetness in her eyes.. Even while she was dying, Gabriela had tried to help her.

Padre David got up and offered Anna his arm. "We'd better get going. People are waiting for us."

"David." Anna hesitated, unsure how to ask her question. "Did - what happened - who took care of burying Gabriela?" Padre David was very still. "I took care of it Anna. Let's go."

She nodded and took his arm. They left the park and strolled up the Avenue Francisco Bilbao a short distance. A left onto Avenue Pedro de Valdivia for a few blocks, then a right and they were on Las Violetas. Anna looked around her, confused.

"What is it, Anna?" said Padre David.

"What?" she said.

"You look puzzled. What's wrong?" Padre David said without breaking his stride. Providencia was one of the old, wealthy neighborhoods of Santiago, where wealth and power combined to create an unobtrusively beautiful environment.

"It's this neighborhood," she said. "What are we doing here?"

"I told you. We're visiting someone."

Anna pointed at the rich and stately houses surrounding them. "But we've never been anywhere like this before."

"Did you think the government only paid

attention to the poor?" He took her arm and guided her into a winding driveway. Passing the walk leading to the front door, he led Anna to a side entrance and rang the bell.

A tall woman of about forty came to the door. She was immaculately dressed in black slacks, a silk blouse, and earrings to match the blouse.

"Padre David. Come in," she said. "Miguel is waiting for you in the library."

"Hello Sylvia," he said. "This is Anna."

Sylvia nodded, then ushered them through a big, airy kitchen that looked as if it had never produced a meal. They passed through a hallway from which they had tantalizing glimpses into other rooms. It looked as if everything belonged in a museum. Sylvia opened the library door. "Miguel, they're here."

A man looked up from his desk when they walked in, and stood up to greet them. Anna's eyes widened when he unfolded himself from his chair. The man was even taller than his wife. He loomed over them, tall and skinny, dressed in gray slacks and a gray pullover that accentuated his height.

"Padre David. It's good to see you again." He held out his hand to Padre David, who took it and then introduced Anna. "Yes, you're the young lady whose husband was arrested."

"Yes," said Anna.

"Please sit down," he said. Anna and Padre David sat in the leather chairs across from the desk. "Could you get us some tea my dear?" he asked his wife. She nodded and disappeared.

"How are you?" Padre David said. Miguel lowered himself into the chair inch by inch. He grimaced, then smiled when he settled into it.

"As you can see, our friends left me with some permanent memories."

"How are the children?" Padre David said. The question seemed innocent enough to Anna, but Miguel's knuckles whitened as his hands clenched the arms of his chair.

"The children are fine," he replied. He smiled again when his wife brought in a tray and put it on the desk. No one spoke while she poured, automatically adding cream and sugar to each cup.

"I'll be out in the kitchen if you need me," Sylvia said. She closed the door behind her and Miguel sighed.

"It's been hard on her," he said.

"They didn't hurt her or the children-" Padre David began.

"No, no," Miguel assured him. "They were all left alone." He turned his attention to Anna. "This must not make any sense to you."

"It does - you were arrested, weren't you?"

"Yes. I was." Miguel spoke reluctantly. "According to Padre David, your husband is being held in the same prison where I was."

"What?" Anna almost leaped out of her chair. Padre David put a hand on her arm, and she subsided. "I'm sorry. But did you know my husband, or see him in the prison?"

"Unfortunately, no," said Miguel. "I was kept in solitary confinement the entire time."

"How long were you there?"

"Just over a year."

"A year," Anna repeated numbly. Romo hadn't even been gone three months and this man had been in for over a year.

"Are you all right, Anna?" asked Padre David. She managed a smile.

"I'm fine. It was just a shock to hear it." She didn't know how to ask what she needed to know. "What did they - how did you stand it?"

Miguel set his cup down and looked directly at Anna. "I didn't have a choice. They weren't willing to let me die. And I had no means of taking my own life."

"But you wouldn't have," said Anna.

"I don't know," he said. "There were times when death would have been a blessing."

Anna held the cup in both hands while she drank. The sweet, milky childhood taste of the tea comforted her.

"Will you tell me about it?" she said.

"Are you sure you want to know?" said Miguel.

"Yes."

He glanced at Padre David, who cast a worried look at Anna, then nodded.

"Very well. My arrest was arranged by one of my business competitors. He wanted the government contracts I'd been getting, so he set up a situation in which I would appear to have cheated the army." Miguel ate one of the little cookies his wife had brought in on the tray, and then swallowed a mouthful of tea.

"Once I was arrested I didn't see daylight again until more than a year later. I never saw anyone unless

172

it was to-," he paused, searching for the right word, "-talk to me. But I never gave them the answers they wanted to hear, so they tried to persuade me." He smiled with grim humor.

"As you can see, I am not a small man. My cell was quite tiny, and I could never stretch out straight on my bunk. The ceiling was very low, so it left me with some permanent problems."

Anna sat her cup down with a jerk and clasped her hands in her lap.

"Don't feel sorry for me, Anna," said Miguel. "I'm one of the lucky ones. I got out, and all I lost was about a hundred pounds." His smile disappeared. "If your husband is still alive, they have probably told him you are dead."

"Why?" she whispered.

"To break him." Miguel watched her with compassion. "I'm sorry. They told me they had killed my entire family. None of it was true, but it almost broke my heart."

"Have some more tea, Anna," said Padre David. She took the cup he poured and downed it in a few gulps. The warmth spread through her cold body.

Taking a deep breath she said, "What should I do?"

"Nothing," Miguel answered flatly.

"I can't do nothing," she said, eyes flashing. He shook his head sadly.

"There is nothing you can do for your husband. Take care of your children and yourself."

She thought about Rico. "But-" she began. Padre David threw her a warning frown and Anna stopped.

"Miguel, what will you do now?" Padre David said.

"We're leaving the country." He looked at the picture of his wife on the desk and smiled. "Sylvia has a sister who lives in Canada. We'll be going to stay with her for a while."

"They'll let you leave?" Anna said.

"Yes. I'm more of an embarrassment here than I would be there."

"When do you leave?" asked Padre David.

"Tonight." Anna and Padre David looked around them in confusion. "We take nothing but one suitcase apiece. So this is goodbye, Padre David." The two men got up and embraced.

"God bless you, Miguel," Padre David said. Miguel smiled his melancholy smile at them and waved as they went out the library door.

They walked several blocks without a word. Anna was the first to speak.

"I want you to find out what you can about Rico's idea, then get Tomas to sit down and talk about it," she said.

"Why don't you talk to Tomas?" Padre David said.

"He'll listen to you."

"Don't assume that because Miguel had a bad time..." Padre David's words trailed off, as if he didn't believe them himself.

"You heard him, David," she said. "We know
174

Romo was in the same prison, and we know they aren't interested in his comfort or well-being."

"Right," he said. "Will you do something for me, too?"

"What?"

"Look for that article. It could be useful."

Anna caught a glimpse of the strain in his face before he had a chance to mask it. She shivered and kept walking.

"I won again, Mama!" Pablo twirled the chair in circles in front of the computer. He stopped his chair by catching Anna's with his bare feet. "Do you want to play now?" He cued her on her response with a negative shake of his head.

"No thanks," she said. "You go ahead." She turned back to the notes she was reading at Romo's desk. She'd been through everything in his desk and file cabinets twice since she got home. There was nothing. Pablo chattered on as he played. Anna ignored him until a name caught her attention.

"-and Juanita told me I'd be able to beat her someday."

"Does Juanita still play with you on the computer?" said Anna. Pablo didn't look up from his game.

"Uh-huh. She's good."

Anna watched him for a few minutes. Did Juanita think Romo's missing article was on the computer? It wasn't. She'd been through every document in his file and they were all innocuous.

"Pablo, does Juanita ever ask you about Papa's work or his files?"

"Nope," he said. Anna frowned. It didn't make sense. "'Course I had to show her which was his stuff on the computer," he added, "So we didn't mess it up." She congratulated herself silently. So Juanita *was* checking the computer.

Could I have missed something? she thought. She laid a hand on Pablo's shoulder. "Querida, I need to use the computer after this game, okay?"

"Sure, Mama." The computer screen suddenly went blue and flashed GAME OVER. Pablo got up. "I could have won. You interrupted me."

"Sorry," said Anna. She switched chairs with him and exited the game. She heard Pablo stand up and move closer to watch her.

"What are you doing?" he said. "I thought you wanted to play?" Anna heard the petulant tone in her son's voice and hid a smile.

"I just want to look up a few things," she assured him, "Then you can have it back." She scanned the root directory and saw nothing unusual. They didn't have much on their computer. Some games and educational programs for the boys. She and Romo used the word processor almost exclusively. There was also a home budget program, but neither of them ever took the time to learn it.

The list of sub-directories in the word processor popped up. She, Romo and each of the boys had their own directories. Checking each of the sub-directories was the work of a few minutes. Anna could hear Pablo shifting from one foot to the other behind her. He was impatient, but he'd have to wait. Only one more directory, hers. She read through the files listed and saw nothing odd. Dates were all pretty much what she'd expect. Damn. Nothing at all.

"I want to try just one more thing, Pablo, then you can get back to your game." He sighed and perched on the arm of her chair. Anna ran through the disk utility and printed out the report. She didn't understand most of it, but maybe it would show if someone had tampered with it. "Okay." She took the report from the printer and moved aside to let Pablo squeeze back in. "It's all yours."

"Thanks." Before he finished saying thanks, Pablo was engrossed in another round of video battle. Anna skimmed the report. There wasn't much. Just disk totals, how much memory used, how much left, lots of disk information she didn't understand.

Her eyes widened. Under disk totals it showed three hidden files. She and Romo had always laughed at the idea of hidden files since they had enough trouble with the ones that were in plain sight, but they'd always shown up on the reports. At least, two of them had. According to the report there was an extra hidden file. That didn't make sense. Computers were always accurate. And neither she nor Romo had ever understood the computer well enough to do that kind of tinkering. Or so she'd thought.

Pablo was still absorbed in his game. She'd have to wait until he went to bed before trying to figure this out. If he saw what she was doing, he might let something slip to Juanita. She was sure this was something Juanita should not see.

Anna went over to the bookshelf and found the computer book. She blew the dust off the top and turned to the index. "Files, hidden..."

Chapter Eighteen

September 23, 1988

"Where is he?" said Anna. She paced back and forth in front of the puma cage at the zoo on Cerro San Cristobal. In spite of being located in the middle of the city, the zoo was deserted, winter not being a popular time for visitors.

"He'll be here," said Padre David. "We were early. Relax." Taking his own advice, he leaned back against the cage railing. It was a healthy distance from the bars, or any paws that might snake out.

Anna stopped in front of him. "Do you think Tomas will go along with it?"

"I don't know," he said.

She resumed her pacing, keeping an eye on both entrances to the cat house. First one, then the other. Padre David glanced at the pumas behind him, then at Anna. He chuckled. Anna glared at him.

"What's so funny?" she said.

"Take a look."

He pointed over his left shoulder. One of the pumas paced back and forth inside the cage, paralleling Anna's pacing. Its tail twitched with every step. In spite of herself Anna grinned at Padre David.

"Are you trying to tell me something?" she said. Her grin faded and she looked at her watch.

"Any luck finding the article?" asked Padre David.

"N-no," she said. She debated the wisdom of letting him know about the hidden files, but decided to wait until she had something definite. She met his searching glance with a blank look. She checked her watch again.

"Here he is," Padre David said. Anna turned to see Tomas coming through the far door. He stopped to read the placard in front of the tigrillo. Then he drifted over to the puma cage.

"What's the occasion?" he asked. He stood a few feet away from Anna and Padre David and observed the pumas.

"First, I want to know why you told David not to talk to me," Anna said.

"I didn't say that," Tomas said.

"Don't quibble. You asked David not to discuss Rico's photograph idea with me. Why?"

"It's too dangerous," Tomas said. Anna shook her head.

"Not good enough," she said. "This meeting is dangerous. All of our meetings are dangerous."

"True. Let's move along," he said. Anna stepped briskly ahead and Padre David and Tomas trailed behind her. They all stopped in front of the quina cage. One wild cat was sleeping, and the other was nowhere in sight. Tomas continued. "Why are you so set on photographs? What do you think you'll accomplish?"

Anna made sure no one was around before she spoke. "If we can prove Romo is in prison, maybe they'll let him out."

"You don't really think it's that simple, do you?" Tomas said in a harsh voice that startled her. Anna had only heard him talk in that tone of voice once before. That had been during the worst fight he and Romo ever had.

"I don't know why you're so angry," she said. "Even if it's not that simple, at least it's something."

"You haven't made contact with Amnesty International, have you?" asked Tomas.

"Of course not, you know that."

"Do you know how to make contact, without endangering yourself and your family? Do you know who to talk to? Do you know -"

"All right Tomas," Anna snapped. "We've established that I don't know anything. How about helping me figure it out?"

The quina got up, stretched and went outside, as if disturbed by the angry voices. Padre David laid a hand on their shoulders and guided them toward the last cage in the building. A tigrillo reclined on his ledge. The only movement he made was the slow blink of his yellow eyes while he watched them.

"Tomas, do you have any connections with Amnesty International?" Padre David said.

"Yes," Tomas replied.

"You do? But that's great," Anna said. "Let's call -"

"Wait a minute, Anna," Padre David said. She waited. Padre David exchanged a long look with Tomas. "You've already talked with them, haven't you Tomas?"

"Yes," he said. He started back to the other end of the cat house.

"You did?" said Anna. She followed him, with Padre David close behind.

"I called a friend of mine right after you told me about Romo's arrest," Tomas said.

"Why didn't you tell me?" she cried. She grabbed his arm and jerked him to a stop. He turned to her. She was shocked by the haggard expression on his face.

"I didn't want to get your hopes up," said Tomas. "Amnesty International couldn't do anything at that point."

"But once it was confirmed that someone had seen him arrested," Padre David said. "Didn't that help?"

"Not really." Tomas' voice sounded tired. "They have a process they follow, which Rico explained to you. What I could tell them wasn't enough."

"Would they consider a photograph of him in prison enough proof?" Anna said.

Tomas shook his head. "I don't know. I can try to find out - that is, if you're sure that's what you want."

"Of course it is," Anna said. "Why not?"

"Because it's still dangerous," Tomas said. "And you have two children to think about, as well as a husband and yourself."

"I don't care about me," she said.

"I know that."

"Find out," Anna said. "That doesn't commit us to anything."

"We don't know for sure that Rico's friends will contact me anyway," Padre David said. "Let's not worry about the danger until we have more information."

Tomas closed his eyes for a second. Anna held her breath. Without his help, she and Padre David couldn't pull it off. Tomas opened his eyes and gave them a weary smile.

"All right, I'll try," he said.

Anna threw her arms around him. "Thanks Tomas. Thank you!"

"We should be going," Padre David said. "Anna, why don't you leave first. I'll be right behind you."

She wondered if it was a ploy to get her out of the way so they could talk alone. It didn't matter. She was going to find a way to get Romo out of that prison. Anna kissed them both on the cheek and left.

Anna raced up the stairs and into the study. She glanced quickly at her watch as she switched the
182

computer on. Only a little over half an hour before Pablo and Luis were due home. She'd been held up on her way back from the zoo by some military parade. At the drop of a hat they closed off busy streets and had parades and maneuvers, regardless of the inconvenience to the Santiago population.

For the last few days Anna had been trying to figure out how to uncover the hidden files in the computer. So far no success.

Once the computer booted up, Anna listed directories and files, added numbers, and tried to decipher memory used and unused. She could feel the sweat trickle along her scalp and down her back. Her eyes burned from the strain of staring directly into the blue computer screen, with its yellow letters. It was no use. She didn't know enough about computers to figure this out, and she couldn't ask anyone else for help.

"Damn!" she said. She sank back against the chair, defeated. What else could she try? She'd read through the manual on the computer, the book on the operating system and even the manual on the word processor. It was impossible.

She checked her watch again. Five more minutes. Then she'd have to get downstairs so the boys wouldn't know what she was doing. They knew she wrote on the computer, but after Pablo's impatience the other night to get back to his game; she didn't want to draw any attention to her computer time.

Maybe if she printed out all the directories and files, she might find something when she went through them later. Anna flipped the printer switch and waited for it to warm up. Better yet, she remembered there was a way to print out the entire screen, instead of just lists. That way she could see the memory and number of files, and more information than she ever wanted to learn.

She shrugged and started printing. It couldn't hurt. Her fingers tapped the printer, ready to yank each page as soon as it was printed. She checked her watch. Two minutes. She swore when her fingers fumbled on the keyboard, quickly corrected the commands and printed out her last sheet.

Anna turned off the computer and printer and pulled the covers back over them, even though they were still warm. She shoved her papers into a folder and dropped it into the desk drawer.

The kitchen door slammed. She dashed to the top of the steps just as Pablo and Luis reached the bottom.

"Stay down there, boys," she said. "I'll come down and get you something to eat."

"I was going to play my computer game," said Pablo. He put one foot on the bottom step. Anna ran down the stairs and swept the two of them along with her into the kitchen.

"Snacks first, then games," she said. "Now how was school today?"

Chapter Nineteen

September 26, 1988

"I was surprised to hear from you this morning," said Anna. Emilio raised an eyebrow.

"Why, my dear?"

"I hadn't heard from you in almost a week. I thought maybe you were out of town."

"No, I've been busy." Emilio led her into the glass-enclosed restaurant. The headwaiter instantly ushered them to a window table with a breathtaking view of Santiago.

Anna sat in the chair Emilio held, and looked out the window. It was a beautiful day - no smog, cold and clear. So clear she could see the university in the shadows of the Andes. Was it her imagination or could she see the little chapel too?

Emilio ordered the wine and dismissed the waiter. "And what have you been doing, Anna?"

Anna turned away from the window. "Not very much. The boys have school and soccer practice. I've been trying to keep up with my work, but it's hard."

"Why is that?" he said.

Anna was surprised. Emilio had never been interested in her personal life before, other than the part that involved him.

The waiter arrived with the wine, and Emilio lifted his glass in a toast. Anna lifted hers and drank.

"It is a simple question," he insisted. "Why is it hard to keep up with your work?"

Anna searched for a glimmer of sarcasm or humor, but he was serious. Did he know about her involvement with the underground?

"I guess it's hard for me to concentrate on anything but my sons sometimes," she said. "Boys of eight and twelve can be a full-time job all by themselves."

"True," he acknowledged. "But you are free all day while they're at school. What do you do then?"

Anna laughed to hide her growing alarm. He must be suspicious, his questions were so pointed.

"I hate to admit it," she said, "But I often go shopping." Emilio looked politely incredulous and she nodded. "I rarely buy, but I'm always hunting for a bargain. It gets to be an obsession."

186

"Yes, I know something about-" Emilio broke off and stared over Anna's shoulder. She turned and saw two women who had just entered the restaurant. It was Juanita, the babysitter, and Maria, Tomas' wife. Anna almost sprayed her mouthful of wine all over the table.

Juanita and Maria were obviously together. Anna turned back to Emilio, trying to compose herself. She didn't have to worry about giving anything away. He wasn't looking at her, he was staring at them as if he'd seen a ghost, and his face was as white as the tablecloth.

"You will excuse me, my dear," he said. There was a tremor in his voice, betraying an emotion Anna couldn't identify. Was it fear or fury? "I have to go see someone for a moment." Abruptly, he left the table.

She watched him intercept the women before the headwaiter reached them. Emilio spoke rapidly and gestured with the controlled fluency Anna knew so well. She was baffled. It was clear that the women knew each other. Could that be dangerous for her? Maria was no friend of hers, and Juanita wasn't to be trusted.

It was also clear that while Maria was intimidated by Emilio, Juanita was not. Anna couldn't hear their words, but something was very wrong. The headwaiter stepped up, but Emilio brushed him aside. Juanita motioned the headwaiter back to them. Emilio said something and Juanita leaned close to him. Her voice was so soft that Anna wouldn't have known she was speaking if she hadn't seen her lips move. Whatever she said hit Emilio like a slap in the face. He straightened, waited until the women were taken to a table by the headwaiter, and stalked back to his own table. Anna gulped her wine. What would he do now?

Emilio sat down opposite her, his eyes glittering in a mask of rage. He reached a trembling hand across the table to Anna.

"My dear, something has come up. Do you mind if we leave without lunch?"

"Of course not, Emilio, whatever you like," she said.

He took a bill from his wallet, tossed it on the table and escorted her from the restaurant. On her way to the door, Anna sneaked a peek at Juanita and Maria. In the instant she caught sight of them, Juanita looked up with a hint of a smile. Anna, embarrassed to be caught staring, looked away immediately.

While she and Emilio rode down in the elevator she tried to make sense of what she had just witnessed. Why was Emilio so upset, and why was Juanita able to tell him what to do? And why had Juanita smiled at her when she was searching Anna's house behind her back? Anna hoped she could talk to Padre David about it tomorrow.

September 27, 1988

"Anna, this is-"

"No names." The harsh whisper of the man cut off Padre David's introductions. The man peered around the ceiling high shelves that crowded the second hand bookstore. Anna wanted to giggle. She knew she should be serious, but the guy sounded right out of a Humphrey Bogart film. The way the three of them were huddled in the narrow aisle added to the farcical element. Padre David frowned at her. He must be reading her mind.

"Sorry," Padre David said. "We were told you

188

might be able to help us with a photography problem." He pulled a book off the shelf and leafed through it as if browsing.

"I can only give you five minutes," said the little man. Anna was astonished to see beads of sweat forming on his brow. His eyes shifted constantly and he turned a book over and over in his hands. "You want pictures of someone, right?"

Padre David and Anna both nodded. Anna tried to speak, but the little man silenced her with a grimace.

"You have forty-eight hours to decide if you want to work with us," he said. "You need to have three people. Are you interested?"

The abrupt question startled Anna. "Aren't you going to give us some details?" she said. "How can I make a decision if I don't know what's involved?"

The little man shrugged his shoulders. "It's up to you. That's all I can tell you now. Have your answer ready when they call." He handed Anna his book, slipped around the corner and disappeared out the front door.

The cover of the book he'd handed her felt slimy. His hands must have been sweating as profusely as his forehead.

"David, what are we going to do?" she asked. She could hear the rising note of hysteria in her voice. Padre David took the book from her hands and replaced it on the shelf.

"I wish he could have told us more too, but I suppose he felt it wasn't safe. Look at this." He gestured to a picture in the book he held and Anna looked at it. It was a book of Audubon illustrations and

189

Padre David had it open to a cardinal. As Anna bent her head over the book pretending fascination, she saw a young woman at the front of the shop glance down the aisle at them.

Anna wilted against the shelves when the girl went down another aisle. Padre David put the book away and drew Anna around the last set of shelves and into the corner.

"We can't stay here," he said. "Go home and think about it."

"Think about what? He didn't tell us anything," Anna protested.

"He told us all we need to know. If you want to take the risk, they'll try to get a photograph of Romo, taken in the prison. You know it will be dangerous. You have to decide if it's worth the risk."

He pushed her gently toward the door. Anna wanted to stay and talk it over with him, and to tell him about yesterday's abortive lunch with Emilio, but as soon as they got outside the door he released her arm.

"I'll tell Tomas, and have him call you," he said. He put a hand on her shoulder and squeezed. "You'll make the right decision, Anna. I'll pray for you."

"Thanks," she said gratefully. He turned around and melted into the noontime crowd.

Anna read the words on the computer screen while she typed. Thoughts of the man in the bookstore plagued her. Forty-eight hours to decide. How could she decide? What if she found the hidden file and it was Romo's article? Maybe it would help her make the decision. Her fingers slowed on the keyboard, then stopped.

190

She rolled her chair over to Romo's desk and dug out the folder of directories and file lists. Her head propped up by her hands, she tried one more time to make some sense of it, to find the key that would unlock the hidden files. The lines of type blurred in front of her eyes.

Anna dragged one of the computer books in front of her and re-read the sections on hidden files. Why did they always tell you what you don't want to know? Why couldn't they explain how to *find* hidden files instead of how to *create* hidden files?

Anna blinked. Would it help if she created a hidden file of her own? That might help her figure out how to track down the other hidden files. She bent over the book with renewed vigor. Puzzling over the technical jargon, she grabbed a pencil and started jotting down notes on the back of her lists.

The phone shrilled. She looked up. There wasn't anyone she wanted to talk to right now. She bent over the book again. The phone kept ringing.

Eleven, twelve, thirteen rings. She shoved her chair back and snatched up the phone.

"What?"

"Anna?"

"Sorry, Tomas, what's up?" she said.

"You sound like I interrupted something." Tomas' familiar voice had an edge to it. "Were you writing?"

"Not exactly. What's up, Tomas?" Anna settled back in her chair.

"Padre David called me a few minutes ago." Anna sat up straight. "He told me about your meeting."

"What do you think?"

"I don't like it," he said. Anna waited for more. When it was clear that Tomas was not going to elaborate, she felt the first twinges of annoyance.

"Why don't you like it?" she asked.

"Don't be sarcastic. I've told you my objections. It's too dangerous."

"So is prison," she said. Tomas didn't respond. "All right. So you don't like it. Will you help us anyway?"

"Why do you want my help?" he said. Anna wanted to scream at him not to be stupid.

"If you talked to David, you know we need three people," she said calmly. "David, you, and me, if you're willing."

"Anna, will you do a favor for me?" Tomas' voice had a pleading note in it that sounded strange to Anna.

"If I can," she said guardedly.

"I'll agree to help you, if that's your final decision."

"That's great, Tomas."

"But - before you give your answer will you think about it?"

"I have been," she said, exasperated.

"No, I mean really think about it," he insisted. "Take a good look at those sons of yours and ask yourself if you're willing to risk their lives on a crazy plan with a slim chance of success." His breathing was uneven on the other end of the line.

"All right, Tomas," she said. "I'll think about it. And I'll call you tomorrow."

She hung up the phone. A picture of Luis and Pablo at breakfast that morning came, unbidden, to her mind. She had managed not to think about the danger to them most of the time. She didn't want to think about it.

Anna went back to her interrupted work at the desk. She studied her notes and rolled back over to the computer. The screen was blank, except for a letter and symbols. She looked at it: C:\>. She checked her notes one more time, typed: attrib *.*., and hit the Enter button. A short list appeared and Anna clenched her fist in the air. Success!

She read down the list carefully:

C:\COMMAND.COM

SH C:\IO.SYS

SH C:\MSDOS.SYS

A C:\CONFIG.SYS

A C:\AUTOEXEC.BAT

A R C:\MENU.DAT

A R C:\MENU.BAK

The two files with "H" next to them were hidden files, according to her book. Anna's heart stopped. Where was the third hidden file? The report had shown three, but only two were here. And they were system files, not documents. She stared at the screen, fighting the urge to pick up the monitor and throw it against the wall.

She forced herself to take deep breaths. There must be something she was missing. What was it? Her eyes narrowed and she looked closely at the list. All of the files listed with attributes were just that, files. None of them was inside a directory. Could Romo have hidden a file inside a different directory?

Anna felt as if she were flying blind. She typed in **DIR** at the prompt and looked at the list of directories. Three games, two educational programs, the word processor, the utility program and the budget package. She tried the word processor directory first, and typed in the magic phrase: `attrib *.*`. A list appeared on the screen. She scanned it, holding her breath. Nothing. The list showed no hidden files.

It didn't make sense. Her head felt light from staring at the computer screen. Romo wouldn't have hidden his writing file in the boys' games or programs. He couldn't. Or could he? She remembered him showing her how she could get into the word processor from any directory, but she'd thought that was a useless idea. What if he'd used it?

She tried the game and educational program directories one after the other. Nothing. She slumped against the back of the chair. There were only two directories left. She almost hated to try them, because if she didn't find anything, she wouldn't know what else to do.

With a sigh she got into the budget program. Neither of them had ever wanted to take the time to learn this one. Too practical. She typed `attrib *.*` and there it was.

H C:\EMILIO.DOC

Anna stared in disbelief. Proof that her husband had lied to her. Had kept a major part of his life a secret from her for years. She'd known it intellectually since Tomas told her, but until this moment it hadn't been real.

She felt a stab of pain in her chest at the

realization of how far apart they had been, even at the beginning of their marriage.

She put the hurt aside for a moment. Finding the file was only part of it. Now she had to change the attribute so it was no longer hidden, and read it. Plenty of time for emotional outbursts later.

Anna read her notes closely. She carefully typed

attrib -H EMILIO.DOC. She pressed Enter, then typed **dir** and pressed Enter. There it was with the other files, no longer hidden. She booted up the word processor and tried to open up the document. It asked for a password.

She grabbed her pile of notes and threw them across the room in a shower of papers. She sat back, trembling, in her chair, unable to move and looked at the computer screen again. Well, she thought grimly, if he could think of a password I guess I can figure it out.

She typed in "Emilio". No good. "Romo". No good. The boys' names, her name, and every name she could think of. Nothing worked.

Anna jumped up and paced around the little study. She could only take three or four steps in any direction, but it helped to be up and moving. She stopped and stared at his desk, as if it could offer some clue. But there was nothing. Her gaze shifted to the painting above the desk. El Greco. *View of Toledo.* His favorite artist and his favorite painting. Dark clouds threatening the city on the hills. Her mind scoffed at the association, but somewhere inside her a kernel of excitement exploded.

She raced over to the keyboard and typed in "ElGreco". The document appeared. She didn't even read it before starting to print it out. She wanted to hide the document on the computer again before anyone else could see it. Then she could read it, pass it on, or burn it.

The printer hummed and she impatiently waited for the last page. Ten pages. With trembling fingers she typed in

attrib +H EMILIO.DOC. When she ran the directory again, the file had disappeared. Hidden from prying eyes. She turned off the computer and settled in the chair to read the article that had changed her life.

The first couple of pages she skimmed, flicking past them, impatient to get to the meat. On the fourth page words leaped out at her. Accident...avalanche...Jack and Kathleen Kelly. The pages dropped to her lap.

Jack and Kathleen Kelly had been her parents. They had died in the avalanche in Chile that had also killed Emilio's wife.

Anna picked up the papers and began reading again from the beginning. This time she didn't skip a word. Her adrenalin surged as she turned the pages. Emilio had been involved with a political splinter group that was considered radical at that time...His work had been to arrange accidents for people who supported Allende, the president, and who were trying to get foreign aid for Chile...Her parents weren't the first, nor were they the last, whose "accidental" deaths had been arranged by Emilio.

My parents were murdered, she thought. And by their best friend. No wonder he wants to find this article. Grief as fresh as the day she'd learned of their deaths swept through her. She could see them vacationing at Portillo as if it were yesterday. Laughing

196

and arguing over who was the best skier. Radiant with their enthusiasm, their joy, and their love for one another.

Her memories were shattered by the peal of the doorbell. Anna checked her watch. It was too early for the boys. It couldn't be Emilio? Where could she hide the article? She folded it in half and stuck it inside GRIMM'S FAIRY TALES.

"I'm coming," she said, running down the stairs. The summons of the doorbell sounded urgent. She yanked the door open and was amazed to find Padre David on the porch.

"Can I come in?" he said, breathing in gasps.

"Of course." Anna stepped back to let him and closed the door. "What is it? Is something wrong?"

"I'm sorry - to come in person but I - didn't want to take - a chance on the phone." Padre David spoke in short bursts while he tried to catch his breath. "I got some news today."

"What - have you heard something about Romo?" she said.

"Yes, and he's fine." Anna sat down abruptly on the steps and he reached out a hand to her. "I didn't want to upset you, but I knew you were trying to decide what to do about the photographs."

"David, tell me," she said. He looked at her gravely, then crowded in beside her on the step.

"A friend called me earlier. He says they're planning to get rid of some of the prisoners."

"But that's good," said Anna. "Does that mean Romo might be released soon?"

"That's not good." Padre David took her hand

in both of his and held it tightly. "They plan to get rid of them by executing them. The plebiscite is just over a week away. If Pinochet gets his 'yes' vote, and another eight years as president, the executions will take care of some loose ends. Anna, Romo is on the list."

Anna moaned and sagged against him. He put an arm around her and held her without a word. She gripped the hand that was still holding hers and rested her head against it. The trembling started in her hands and spread through her entire body. "After all this time," she said. "Why now?"

"I don't know, Anna, but I knew you needed to know."

Anna raised her head and controlled the trembling with an effort. "You're right, and thanks." She stood up and opened the door. "You'd better go. It isn't safe for you to stay here."

"Will you be all right?" he said.

"I have to be." He nodded, kissed her forehead and left.

Later that night she paced quietly through the downstairs so as not to wake the boys. She wanted to kill Emilio. He murdered her parents. Romo was about to be executed thanks to him. She prowled through the first floor of the house, living room to hall, hall to kitchen, then back again. She couldn't stop moving. Every instinct urged her to do something, to put a fist through the wall, and she couldn't. I want to grab an Uzi and blow his brains out, she thought.

She was on her fourth trip through the hall when the doorbell rang. It had to be Emilio. What the hell was that son of a bitch doing here after midnight?

She stopped. She leaned her forehead against the door for a moment, trying to gather her strength to stay calm. She opened the door. Her stomach heaved at the sight of him. Damn you, she thought. You bloody murderer. I can't do this anymore! But she was silent. Her hands curved into claws. In her imagination she could see the red furrows her nails would dig through his cheeks. But she hid her hands behind her back and was silent.

Emilio didn't wait for an invitation. He brushed past her and into the hall. Anna stifled a protest. He looks almost as bad as I do, she thought. I wonder why? Not that I care.

"What's wrong?" she said.

His answer was to grab her by the arm and drag her upstairs. Anna stumbled on the top step. Damn, she thought. She didn't want to wake Luis. Pablo could sleep through a train wreck, but Luis was a light sleeper.

The instant Anna closed the bedroom door, Emilio grabbed her again. Jesus Christ! she thought. He's going to kill me. Fear choked off her breath. Her skin crawled at the touch of his hands. He ripped her blouse off and flung his pants in a corner. This wild man wasn't the Emilio she knew. The Emilio she knew took his pleasure deliberately. Folded his socks and shorts and placed them in a neat pile. Tonight he tore his clothes off, threw her on the bed and was on top of her and inside her in seconds.

Murderer, she screamed inside her head. You bloody murderer. All day long the scream had been building. But she didn't scream alone. In her mind, the entire country screamed with her. The people at MacDonald's, who had watched a man being dragged away by soldiers, and did nothing. Gabriela's neighbors, who had been afraid to investigate the shouts of the soldiers who were brutalizing her. Anna heard the screams of every helpless bystander in Chile demanding release. But there was no release.

"Mama?"

Luis' voice was soft, outside her door.

Oh God, she prayed. Keep him out of here. Emilio's mouth devoured hers. She couldn't speak. She wanted to scream at Luis, Stay out. But she was silent.

Luis opened the bedroom door. She saw his white face over the broad expanse of Emilio's back and wrenched her mouth free.

"Go back to bed, Luis," she said. He stared at them. Emilio turned his head.

"Get out!" he roared. Luis bolted.

Wait, she wanted to cry. I can explain! Anna heard his door slam. She held her hand out in mute appeal, but Luis was gone. Emilio seized her outstretched hand and gave a final thrust.

Anna couldn't breathe. He was still on top of her, his face buried in her hair. His breathing slowed against her body. They were both soaked in sweat.

Emilio got off. He didn't look at her. He got dressed and left without a word.

The memory of the expression on Luis' face, sent a hot flush of shame over her body. He was already so angry with her, and there was nothing she could say.

Anna forced herself to get out of bed and put on a robe. She glanced in the mirror. Her hair was a mess, but it would have to do.

200

The walk to Luis' door was all too short. She knocked. There was no response. "Luis," she said softly. Nothing. Anna tried the door, but he had locked it. She rested her forehead against the door and suppressed the urge to batter it down. There was no point in pressing the issue tonight. They were both too raw to handle it.

On the way back to her room, she stopped and sat down on the top step, the one she'd tripped on. She leaned back against the wall and closed her eyes. What now?

Chapter Twenty

September 28, 1988

Anna knocked on the door and tried the handle. It was still locked. She knocked again and called.

"Luis, time to get up." She heard movements inside the room, but he didn't come to open the door.

Pablo grinned at her on his way to the bathroom and she ruffled his hair when he scampered past. At least one of her sons was happy with her. Luis had made it clear he wasn't coming out until she left her vigil, so Anna went down to the kitchen to start breakfast. With every move her body protested. She had sat on that top step for hours, hoping Luis would open his door, and reluctant to return to her bedroom and the nightmare memory of Luis' dazed expression. Eventually she had fallen asleep, sprawled on the steps and the hall floor. At about five in the morning the cold had awakened her, and she went down and made a pot of coffee.

She checked the kitchen clock. Seven-thirty. The boys had plenty of time. She poured the coffee and got out bowls and cereal for them. It was her second pot of coffee. Anna sat down at the table, a steaming cup in front of her. Would Luis talk to her this morning? Would he tell Pablo what he'd seen last night? Would he listen to her explanation? Explanation. What in the world could she say to him? Her mind had been running on the same track for hours, but she was no closer to an answer.

Pablo charged into the kitchen, shirttail flying. "Come here, young man," Anna said. He shifted from one foot to the other while she tucked in his shirt. "Have some cereal."

He chatted to her while he ate. Anna listened and responded with half an ear, waiting for Luis' footsteps. When he finally came down she never heard him until he appeared, entering silently in his sneakers. Anna was so startled she spilled the milk she was trying to pour for Pablo.

"Mama!" Pablo's surprised exclamation recalled her attention. She mopped up the spilled milk and apologized to Pablo.

"Do you want some cereal, Luis?" she said. Maybe if she behaved normally, he'd follow her cue. He ignored her and fixed himself a bowl. Pablo finished his breakfast and Anna sent him upstairs to brush his teeth. Luis couldn't ignore her indefinitely. Even a fight would be better than this silence. She'd have to say something.

"I'd like to talk to you about last night," she said.

Luis looked at her for the first time. His face was expressionless. "I hate you," he said. He turned to his cereal.

Anna felt as if he'd kicked the breath out of her. He was so calm, so cold. She had to get through to him.

"Luis, you don't understand," she began.

"I don't *want* to understand," he shouted. He jumped up from the table and glared at her. He waited for her to continue, then shook his head when she didn't. "I hate you," he yelled. Tears glittered in his eyes and he banged his chair against the table and ran out of the room.

Anna dropped her head into her hands. She was losing everything. It was beyond tears, beyond fixing.

"Mama, don't cry." Pablo's childish treble brought her head up.

"I'm not," she assured him. "I was just tired, that's all."

He patted her shoulder. "Should I pray for you, Mama, so you feel better?" he said.

She caught him in a tight embrace. "Yes, Pablo. Pray for Mama."

"Tomas?" Anna's hands held the kitchen phone in a death grip. Pablo and Luis had gone to school, and she was burning her bridges.

"Anna? What's wrong?" he said.

"I have a message for David. Tell him to go ahead."

"Anna, can we talk about this?"

"No," she said. "Just tell him."

"What happened?"

"Nothing. Everything's fine." Anna knew her voice sounded shaken and almost hysterical, but she didn't care.

"I'll be there in fifteen minutes."

"Tomas, don't-" The dial tone interrupted her. She hung up the phone. It didn't matter. There was nothing Tomas could do to change her mind.

A brisk tapping sounded on the kitchen door. Anna opened it. She would not get hysterical.

"Come in, Tomas. Do you want some coffee?"

"Sure." He stood inside the door. She could feel him watching her while she got the coffee. She knew he was looking for some clue as to what was going on. It didn't matter. Nothing mattered but finding some way out of this impossible trap they were in.

"You wasted your time coming over here," she said.

"I don't think so." They sat down at the table. Anna didn't give him a chance to talk.

"It's very simple," she said. "Tell David I want to go ahead. He's to let those people know and tell me what I'm to do."

"Why? What's happened that makes it so urgent?" said Tomas. He watched her out of the corner of his eye, while he added milk to his coffee.

"They only gave me forty-eight hours to decide," she said, fencing. "My time's about up."

"There's more to it than that." Tomas waited, then pressed. "What's wrong, Anna?"

Anna went over to the refrigerator and opened the freezer. Her movements were contained, with no sign of the distress she felt from her encounter with Luis. She got out a box of frozen popsicles, pulled a sheaf of papers from the box and handed it to Tomas.

"Read this," she said. While he read, she cleaned up the kitchen. The quiet was punctuated by the clatter of dishes and Tomas' occasional exclamations. When he was finished, she sat down across from him.

"Where did you get this?" Tomas said.

"Romo had hidden it on the computer. That's the file Emilio was looking for. That's why Romo was arrested."

"I'm sure you're right," he said. "What are you going to do with it - blackmail Emilio?"

"No." Anna shook her head. "If he knew I had it we'd all be dead. It's too late for that now."

"Too late? Why? And what does this have to do with your decision this morning?"

"Wherever the photographs are sent, I want copies of that article sent too."

"Why?" said Tomas.

"Someone might publish it. It might discredit

Emilio. Romo might get out." For the first time Anna allowed herself the luxury of showing her emotions. "I know it's a long shot, Tomas, but I have to try," she pleaded. "Romo was going publish it anyway."

"All right, but I could probably get this out without the photographs. Wouldn't that work just as well?"

Anna traced the outline of the cup with her index finger. She didn't know how much Padre David had told Tomas, but he'd have to know anyway.

"David came here yesterday afternoon-"

"That was stupid! It's dangerous for both of you." Tomas glowered at her with impotent rage.

"He came to tell me that Romo is on a list of people to be executed after the plebiscite next week."

"What?" His eyes were wide; it was obvious Tomas was hearing it for the first time. His rage transformed into comprehension. "That's why you want to do it," he said. Anna nodded. He frowned. "I still don't like it, Anna."

Luis' face swam before her eyes, full of pain and hatred. "Neither do I, but there isn't any choice." Her voice was tight. "I have to do it, and it has to be done now."

Tomas cocked his head at her. "Are you sure that's all there is to it?"

"What else would there be?" she asked. She willed her voice to remain calm.

"I don't know." He studied her for a moment. She returned his look steadily. "All right. I'll get back in touch with you."

Anna walked him to the door. When he turned

to say goodbye, she was surprised to see a film of moisture over his eyes. Before she could say anything he waved and was out the door.

Chapter Twenty-One

September 29, 1988

"Are you sure this is the right place?"

Anna shuddered at her first glimpse into the stark interior of the deserted warehouse. Wooden packing crates were piled haphazardly, some stacked in pyramids over twenty feet high and others scattered on the dusty planks that served as a floor. Irregular shafts of light cut through dirty windows high above her head, adding to the eerie atmosphere.

Padre David and Tomas explored the warehouse, debating the relative merits of possible hiding places. They spoke in hushed tones, though there was no one around to hear them.

Padre David pointed to a cul de sac between two of the larger pyramids of crates. "This is big enough for the three of us," he said.

Tomas shook his head. "We'd be trapped in there," he said.

"You didn't answer my question," said Anna. "Are you *sure* this is the right place?" She didn't want to sound like a spoiled brat, but the place scared her.

"This is it," said Padre David. "I was told not to worry if our contact was late. It might be difficult for them to get here exactly on time."

Tomas examined the door again. It was the only entrance or exit to the outside that was unlocked. Anna was sure of that, because Tomas had already tried the other doors several times. He circled the first floor of the warehouse again, checking in every corner and behind every box.

"What is it, Tomas?" asked Anna. "You're making me nervous."

"I don't know," said Tomas. "I kept thinking someone was following us, but I didn't see anyone." Anna looked behind her.

"I don't think so," said Padre David. "We didn't meet until we got to the metro station, we didn't sit together on the bus. And we were the only people who got on at our stop."

"Why aren't they here yet?" said Anna. She found it difficult to speak softly and hear her own words over the beating of her heart. "What if they don't show up?" She leaned against a tall crate, her arms wrapped tight around herself.

"It will be fine," said Tomas. "Once we get the film, there are three of us meeting three different contacts in three different parts of the city. Three chances for success."

"Are you sure we should send the story too?" asked Padre David. "The film's risky enough, but the story can be traced directly to Anna. Why couldn't you use your regular courier?"

"It would have taken too much time the usual way," said Tomas. "And it's too late now. Romo's article is the reason he was arrested. My contacts are salivating over it."

"Who wants it?" asked Anna. Tomas shook his head.

"Can't tell you that. It's too dangerous for everyone involved. Just trust me, that if the film and the story get through, all hell will break loose."

Anna contracted her brows. "I'm not sure I like the sound of that, Tomas. What if you make things worse?"

"From what you told me, things can't get much worse. I'm just trying-"

"What *are* you trying to do?" All three of them whirled at the sound of a woman's voice. Maria, Tomas' wife, stood just inside the door.

"Maria, what are you doing here?" exclaimed Tomas. He started toward her, then stopped abruptly when she raised her arms and pointed a .22 caliber pistol at him.

"Even here you follow her and protect her," Maria said bitterly. "Well I heard everything, and none of you will get away with it." The double click of Maria cocking the pistol and snapping the safety off sent fear rocketing through Anna's entire body.

"What did you hear?" said Padre David. His voice was calm and soothing. Maria laughed, a high, shrill cackle. It sent chills down Anna's spine.

"A priest. How did you two get him to help you?" She bared her teeth at Anna, but kept the gun trained on Tomas. "Or do you share your favors with him too?" Her words were calm, but the note of hysteria was unmistakable. Anna stood, frozen, and finally found her voice.

"Maria," she said, "Tomas and I never-"

"Don't bother," said Maria. "Save it for Emilio."

"What?" Tomas snapped. Maria turned to him.

"That's right, querida. Emilio asked me to keep an eye on you a long time ago. I always knew you had a thing for Anna, I just didn't know how far you'd go."

"Maria, Anna and I have never been more than friends," insisted Tomas. Maria laughed wildly. It was clear that nothing they could say would change her mind. She was too far gone in her paranoia.

"I am the one who has met with Anna," said Padre David. "I've been helping her in her husband's absence."

"Right," agreed Maria. "Helping her carry on an affair with my husband. Emilio told me all about it."

Anna exchanged startled glances with Padre David and Tomas. Regardless of the absurdity of Maria's claims, it was clear that Emilio had been paying much closer attention to Anna's activities than any of them had realized. Anna glanced at Tomas again. How would he respond to Maria's accusations? Their eyes met, he reddened and looked away. She couldn't believe it. Maria wasn't completely crazy. Tomas did have feelings for her and she'd never suspected. It explained a lot.

"Bitch!" screamed Maria. Anna's attention swung back to her. She knew Maria had seen the revealing look. "You know, I don't think I'll call Emilio just yet," said Maria, her voice screeching higher and higher. Padre David edged out of Maria's line of sight and crept closer to her, inch by inch.

Maria screamed foul names and horrible accusations at Anna. Anna didn't move, aware that it would take very little to push her over the edge, and aware of the pistol in her hand.

"You'll never have him you whore!" Maria whipped the pistol around and pointed it at Anna's head. Tomas tackled Anna and knocked her to the floor. His body shielded her, but out of the corner of her eye she could see Padre David grab Maria's hands. They fought for control of the gun. A shot rang out. Anna struggled to get up. Tomas was dead weight on top of her. Maria slipped on a puddle of blood and fell heavily against Padre David. Who was hurt? Whose blood was it? Maria's insane fury appeared to equal Padre David's strength. Two more shots rang out. Padre David and Maria collapsed into a heap.

"Get off, Tomas," screamed Anna. He rolled to one side and they both scrambled across the floor. Tomas lifted Padre David into his arms. There was a small bullet hole over his heart. He was dead. The gun lay abandoned on the floor. Anna picked it up. It was small, and heavier than she'd expected. The metal was warm from the hands that had been fighting over it.

A groan from Maria made them turn to her. She tried to sit up, and only succeeded in bracing herself on one elbow. "Why couldn't you ever love me?" she said to Tomas with a grimace of pain. The question sapped her remaining strength. Her eyes closed and she fell back. Tomas laid Padre David carefully on the floor and made the sign of the cross over him. Then he leaned over to feel Maria's pulse.

"They're both dead," he said.

Anna felt numb. "What do we do?"

"We have to hide their bodies."

"Tomas!"

"I'm serious," he said. "They're dead. We still have work to do." He pointed to the cul de sac whose protection he'd rejected earlier. "Help me drag them over there. No one will notice them."

Anna pulled herself up, holding onto the crate beside her, the pistol still gripped tightly in her hand. It was unbelievable. His wife and one of his best friends had just killed each other and he was worried about hiding the bodies. This wasn't the Tomas she knew.

"Give me the gun," he said, still on his knees. She laid it silently in his outstretched hand, and watched him snap on the safety and tuck it in the back of his waistband. He turned back to the bodies and gave her an exasperated shake of the head. "Anna, if you can't help, get out of my way." He got to his feet. She stepped back while he picked up Maria and laid her between the crates.

"How can you?" she cried. "How can you be so cold-blooded?" Tomas straightened up and met her eyes with a grim look.

"We still have a job to do. Now we only have two chances instead of three that it will work. Are you still interested in saving your husband?" Anna blinked. She'd forgotten all about it. Romo. Photographs in prison. She nodded. Tomas shrugged. "Then what
214

choice do we have?"

He started to drag Padre David's body over by Maria's, when the door creaked. They both jumped.

It was Rico. Anna breathed a sigh of relief. Tomas tried to pull her behind a pile of crates, but she jerked away from him. Rico took one horrified look at the body lying face down on the floor and bolted for the door.

"Rico, wait!" said Anna. He turned back, his hand on the door, ready to flee. The lines of tension in his face slackened when he recognized Anna, but he froze again when he looked down and saw a body.

"I have to get out of here," he said. Anna skirted Padre David's lifeless form and went to Rico. She brushed away Tomas' attempt to restrain her.

"It's all right Rico. Tomas and I are here to get the film." She tried to keep him focused on her and not on the body. "Do you have the film?"

"Yes. What happened?"

"Nothing to do with you," said Anna. "The woman is Tomas' wife, who thought he was involved with me. She followed him, tried to shoot us, and Padre David stepped in."

"Padre David," Rico repeated. He went over and knelt down beside the body. Padre David's face had a waxy look when Rico turned him over. Rico looked up at Anna, his face working. "He's dead." Anna knelt down beside him and embraced the fat little man.

"We need to get out of here," Tomas reminded them. Anna got to her feet and stood protectively over Rico and Padre David.

"Don't be so cold," she said. "Padre David was

your friend too, or at least I thought so."

"You know he was, but we don't have much time," said Tomas. He glanced at his watch. "We're still on schedule, but not if we don't get moving. Someone might have heard the shots and called the police."

"He's right," said Rico. He labored to raise his bulk from the floor, and Anna and Tomas both reached down to help him. Rico brushed off his jacket and pulled out two rolls of film from an inner pocket. "Here it is." Anna and Tomas each took a roll.

"Anna, you go first," said Tomas. "I'll take off after you."

"What about the third roll?" she asked.

"Do you know where it was to go?" said Rico.

"Yes," said Tomas. "Padre David told me."

"Tell me, and I'll take it."

"I don't think that's such a good idea," said Tomas.

"Don't worry. My size is an advantage," Rico said with a bitter smile. "No one believes that anyone this fat could be smart or dangerous."

"Could we give him David's copy of the article too?" asked Anna. Tomas frowned. She waited, silently pleading with him to take advantage of every chance they had to get the film and article smuggled out.

"All right," Tomas said. "But Anna, you get out of here while I tell him where he's going."

"Good luck Rico," said Anna. She kissed him on the cheek. "Good luck Tomas. I'll see you tomorrow as we planned." Tomas didn't acknowledge the kiss on the cheek she gave him.

Anna turned back at the door to look at the lifeless bodies of Maria and Padre David one more time. She hesitated, and Tomas hissed, "Get going!" She slipped through the door and out of the warehouse.

When she got outside, Anna was surprised to find the chilly night air warmer than the cold dead air inside the warehouse. She checked carefully in every direction before leaving the protective shadows of the building. No one was in sight. The light from the streetlamps made her feel exposed, and she headed south on San Eugenio at a fast clip. The warehouse was a short distance from Estacion Nunoa, and she could hear the sounds of squealing train brakes and rumbling engines.

She hurried along, grateful for the silence of her sneakers. In the inner pocket of the sheepskin-lined jacket were the precious film and papers. If only no one would try to stop her.

An intersection appeared abruptly. Anna slowed to look back at the warehouse before turning east on Calle 2. Her heart almost stopped. Flashing lights pulled up in front of the warehouse, and in the headlights she could make out Rico's short, round body. One chance out of three, gone. He appeared to struggle in the grip of several uniformed men. She strained to see more, but there was no way to tell if they'd caught Tomas. A car slowly rolled in her direction, and Anna started running.

Lungs heaving, she followed the turns of Calle 2, trying to convince herself they hadn't seen her. Thighs burning, she slowed to a walk. If she showed up at her meeting place frantic and out of breath, it might scare her contact off. Here was Los Jazmines. Only a few blocks to go.

Her breathing under control, Anna turned east on Carlos Dittborn. No flashing lights or patrolling cars so far. What if Tomas had been caught too? If Emilio found out before she got back, Pablo and Luis might not be there when she got home. She gave herself a mental shake. Time enough to worry about that when her package was delivered.

There it was. Avenida Marathon, and behind that, the specter of the Estadio Nacional. It had been returned to its original purpose of soccer stadium and entertainment venue many years ago. But Padre David had told her about the hundreds who had been detained and tortured there in the weeks following the coup. Twenty-five years later, in the recesses of her imagination, Anna could hear the screams, the weeping, and worst of all, the dull thud of blows that maimed and killed.

Legs trembling, she crossed the street and started down the stadium road. Before she went ten feet, a man stepped out of the shadows.

"I'm looking for tickets to the game this weekend," he said. Anna struggled to remember her response.

"Yes - ah, I hear that Catholic University has a good team. I have an extra pair of tickets." Her eyes strained to see in the gloom, but the man was careful to keep the light behind him.

"May I see your tickets?" he said.

Anna drew the envelope that held the film and article from her inner pocket and handed them to him. He nodded.

"Thank you. These will be quite satisfactory."

He slipped back into the shadows without

another word. Anna reached out a hand, then let it drop. He was doing his part. She knew Tomas would be furious if she didn't follow her directions to the letter.

She went back to Avenida Marathon and turned north. She was to catch the bus on Avenida Grecia, take it to the metro station at Parque O'Higgins, and take that to Plaza Banquedano. The walk to Avenida Grecia was a battle. Her instructions versus her need to go back and find out what had happened to Tomas and Rico. It was ridiculous, because there was little chance they'd still be there, and if they were, it meant that they'd missed their contacts. And she'd seen Rico in those headlights. He'd never have been able to get away.

A bus pulled up right after she reached the bus stop. It was almost empty, a second miracle. She stared out the windows at the lights flashing by. At the metro station she watched for Tomas, but she wasn't sure what direction he was to travel to meet his contact. She got on the train, wondering about Tomas and Rico, Pablo and Luis. Their names played like a broken record in her mind. Tomas, Rico. Pablo, Luis. Tomas, Rico. Pablo, Luis

When she exited the metro station at Banquedano, the streets were alive with people and cars. She crossed the river into Bellavista, where she'd parked, again according to instructions. She ignored the occasional catcall or whistle. Music blared from nightclubs, and couples strolled along the streets, absorbed in each other.

Once behind the wheel of her Land Rover, Anna closed her eyes and let her head fall back against the headrest. She had to go to the bathroom. With a groan she put her key in the ignition and checked her watch. Ten o'clock. In Bellavista, the night had just begun.

Chapter Twenty-Two

September 30, 1988

Anna entered the stone church. She stopped inside the door and gave her eyes a chance to adjust to the dim light. A handful of people were scattered through the wooden pews, most of them kneeling in prayer. She glanced over at the confessional and compressed her lips. Why had Padre David, the good priest, the loving priest, been killed? Why not Padre Vincent, the coward?

Her eyes adjusted to the dim church light, and Anna dipped her fingers in the holy water and made the sign of the cross. Tomas was nowhere in sight. It was only quarter to twelve, but he'd said he'd meet her at the noon Mass.

Anna started down the aisle. The clacking of her boots reverberated through the church. She stopped and genuflected five rows from the back, entered the pew and left a small space beside her. Enough for Tomas to be able to ask her to move over, but not enough to encourage anyone else.

She closed her eyes and bowed her head in what would pass for prayer. Would Tomas show up? Had he made his delivery? What happened to Rico? Her heart thudded an irregular rhythm with every question.

"Excuse me." The whispered plea broke into Anna's prayers. Her head flew up and she looked right into Tomas' eyes. His face gave no signs of recognition. Anna nodded and shifted over in the pew to give him room. Tomas knelt beside her. A sideways glance at him got only a shake of the head in response.

Shuffling feet and thumping kneelers made Anna look up. How long had her head been down? The handful of people had grown to a few dozen, and Padre Vincent was up on the altar starting Mass. She and Tomas stood with everyone else.

"Are you okay?" whispered Tomas. His words were all but inaudible under the responses of the crowd. "Did you get through?"

"Yes. How about you?" Her hands gripped the pew in front of her while she waited for his reply.

"Glory to God in the Highest, and peace to his people on earth," mumbled the congregation.

"I got there," he said. "My contact never showed."

Anna stared at him. He picked up a missalette

and handed it to her. They both joined in the end of the prayer.

"With the Holy Spirit, in the glory of God the Father. Amen."

Three chances for success had seemed more than enough last night. But Maria had shown up and Padre David had been shot. Then Rico was captured. Now Tomas reported that his contact had never showed. Anna wondered irrelevantly why her feet and hands felt so numb. Her fingers worried the missalette during the readings and the homily. What if it had all been for nothing? Her contact might not have made it through either. Or he might have been a plant. What a mess.

Padre Vincent and the crowd started droning the Creed.

"We believe in one God, the Father, the Almighty-"

"We'd better not see each other for a while," Tomas muttered.

"What?"

"-We believe in one Lord, Jesus Christ-"

"Remember, Maria was working for someone we both know." Anna forgot about pretense and stared at him again.

"What about Rico?" she whispered urgently. "And how did you get away last night? We have to talk." He nodded toward the altar and they both joined in for a few phrases.

"-We acknowledge one baptism for the forgiveness of sins. We look for the resurrection of the dead-"

"Don't worry about it, Anna, just wait till I call you."

White-hot fury seared through Anna's veins. She was tired of waiting. The urge to wrench the kneeler out of the floor and bash Tomas over the head was overwhelming. The sheer absurdity of the desire brought Anna back to a semblance of sanity. Tomas was in as bad a position as she was. His wife was dead. Did he report her missing, or would he wait till they told him they'd found the body? She thought of his face when Maria had accused them of being lovers. She'd never known he cared. He was Romo's best friend.

"-lead us not into temptation, and deliver us from evil-"

Anna went to communion and returned to her seat. Tomas went up and received communion, then left the church without returning to the pew. She watched him go and wondered how he'd feel about the news she hadn't had a chance to share. Emilio was back in town. She had to see him tonight. His secretary had called before Anna left for church, to say that he'd pick her up for dinner at seven. Would he mention Luis breaking in on them the other night? Who would take care of burying Padre David?

"May Almighty God bless you, the Father, the Son, and the Holy Spirit. Amen."

Anna looked up to see a group of old ladies, lace mantillas on their heads, gather in the front pews of the church. They were beginning another of their interminable rosaries. Anna made the sign of the cross, got up and left.

Pablo and Luis erupted into the kitchen in the midst of a hot argument.

"Boys!" Anna's sharp tone silenced them. "Close the door," she said. Luis pushed the kitchen door shut and looked down at the floor. "Pablo, why don't you take some milk and cookies and go upstairs."

"Mama, that's not fair," he protested.

"You can play on the computer. I need to talk to Luis."

Pablo dropped his books on the kitchen table. He poured himself a glass of milk, grabbed a handful of cookies, and left the room with a hearty sigh.

"Do you want anything to eat or drink?" Anna said. Luis shook his head.

She'd decided to talk him about Emilio, but now that he was here she didn't know how to begin. He was still barely speaking to her.

"Sit down," she said. She sat next to him, her heart in her mouth, praying he'd be able to understand.

"I know you're still upset about what happened - that night - with Emilio." Anna stopped. She didn't know how to do this. Her face burned. She laced her fingers together and spoke slowly and distinctly. "I want you to understand-"

"I understand," he said, his face twisted with hate. "You're sleeping with Uncle Emilio."

She couldn't stop herself.

"Your father didn't go away on an assignment. He was arrested."

Luis' head snapped up. "What?"

"Emilio had him arrested," Anna said. "He

threatened to kill your father and torture you and Pablo if I didn't sleep with him. I couldn't let anything happen to you."

"Since Papa's been gone?" he said. She nodded, unable to speak. Spasms of anger crossed his face. His fists were clenched. "*Uncle* Emilio did this to you." His eyes met hers for the first time, dark with adult bitterness. "I'll kill him," he said.

"Luis, you can't," she said frantically. "You don't understand. If Emilio finds out that I've told you, he'll kill your father."

Luis stared at her. He frowned. "Mama, are you - all right?" She nodded, not trusting herself to speak. Tears appeared in Luis' eyes, he put his arms around his mother. His slender frame shook with sobs while he clung to her. She wanted to cry with him, but she couldn't. It was important for her to maintain control and keep him in check and safe.

"It'll be all right, Luis," she said. She pulled back to look at him.

"What about Papa?" he asked. She wiped the tearstains from his cheeks and hugged him. She wished he could be upstairs playing computer games instead of dealing with this.

"I'm doing what I can."

"Can I help?"

"No, it's too dangerous," she said.

His face closed again and he stepped back, arms folded. "You're still going to sleep with him aren't you?"

"I have to. It's the only way to keep all of us safe."

226

His eyes were black with anger.

"You could stop it if you want to," he raged. "You don't love Papa any more." He ran out of the room.

Anna looked after him, appalled. What had she done? Not only had she burdened him with adult responsibility, but she had also forced him to watch her go out with Emilio, knowing she would sleep with him again.

If he attacked Emilio, it would be a disaster. Luis would never do anything like that. Would he?

Emilio's hand grasped Anna's elbow firmly. He guided her across the crowded dance floor to a table for two against the far wall. Anna sat down, grateful for the plants that protected her from prying glances. Luis had stayed in his room since their talk. At least he hadn't confronted Emilio.

She caught a flicker of emotion in Emilio's face before he sat down. If she didn't know him better, she'd say it was fear. He'd been strange ever since he'd picked her up. They'd hardly exchanged ten words, and he'd only given her a peck on the cheek. Part of her was relieved, but under the circumstances his behavior was disturbing.

"May I order for both of us?" Emilio asked her. She nodded and watched him. He was firm and decisive with the waiter. Maybe she was imagining things.

"Did you have a good trip?" she said. His eyebrows flew up.

"Who told you I went on a trip?"

"I-I think you did," said Anna. His eyebrows

relaxed and she could see him force a smile.

"Of course. I forgot." He lit a thin, brown cigar and puffed for a minute. Anna tried not to show her surprise. Emilio had never smoked in front of her before. "How are the boys?"

"Fine," said Anna. "Pablo's excited about his soccer team winning at school." She kept up a flow of inconsequential chatter, aware that Emilio wasn't listening to her. It was clear that he didn't intend to answer her question about his trip, and equally clear that something was wrong. Could he know about Padre David and Maria? He wouldn't be so calm if he did. Or would he, was he trying to trap her?

By the time the waiter brought their after-dinner coffee, Anna was alarmed. Whatever it was, anything that could affect Emilio to the point that he ignored her was serious. She wasn't sure she wanted to know, but her imagination was running wild.

Familiar strains of music drew Anna's attention to the dance floor. The local band had been playing dance music all night, but they had switched to a folk tune.

"That's the cueca, isn't it?" said Anna.

"Yes," he said without looking.

She remembered the couple that had performed it at the fiesta on Emilio's estate. In spite of her concern about Emilio's behavior, Anna watched, fascinated, when a woman came out in costume and danced. She was doing the traditional movements of the cueca, but without a partner. Anna was puzzled. The folk dance was a courting ritual, meant to be performed by both a man and a woman.

"Why is she dancing alone?" Anna wondered

out loud. Emilio swore under his breath and slammed his glass on the table so hard it shattered. Their waiter rushed over to clean up the mess and Emilio pushed him aside. She felt a spasm of apprehension in the pit of her stomach. His anger etched deep lines in his face, and for the first time Anna noticed his age showing.

"Come on." He rose abruptly. Without waiting for a response, he threw several bills down on the table, grabbed Anna's hand, and dragged her around the perimeter of the dance floor and out to the waiting limo.

Inside the car, Anna waited in vain for an explanation. It made no sense for him to be angry over a dance, but she couldn't think of anything else that could have caused his outburst. Emilio ordered the driver to take them to her house. She watched him out of the corner of her eye, but didn't speak for fear of precipitating another explosion. The driver pulled up in front of the house and she hesitated.

"Tell Juanita I'm waiting," snapped Emilio. Anna murmured good night and climbed out of the car, her head spinning. He didn't seem angry with her, but what was going on?

When Anna entered the front door, Juanita came into the hall from the kitchen. She took one look at Anna and said, "What's wrong? Where's Emilio?"

"In the car," said Anna. The need to talk outweighed caution. "It was the strangest thing."

"What?"

"Some woman danced the cueca at the restaurant tonight. But she did it alone - without a partner." Anna suddenly realized she was talking to

Juanita, another of Emilio's hirelings. She also remembered Emilio waiting in the car. "You'd better go, he said to tell you he's ready."

"That's all right," said Juanita in a crisp voice. "What did he do when the woman danced?"

"Nothing," said Anna. "He didn't even notice until I asked him why she was doing it. Then he got furious. He stormed out." Anna knew it didn't make sense for her to be asking Juanita, but she did it anyway. "Why did he do that, and what did it mean?"

"I'm not sure why he did it," said Juanita. "You don't know what it means?"

"The dance? Well, it's a courting dance, but what does it mean-"

"-when someone dances it alone," Juanita finished. She straightened almost imperceptibly. "It means that her partner is one of the disappeared."

Anna smothered an exclamation. What did Juanita know about the disappeared?

Juanita continued as if she hadn't noticed Anna's reaction. "She's dancing for someone who was arrested, or murdered, someone who's missing."

"How do you know that?" said Anna.

"Don't talk to Emilio about it again, Anna." Juanita started out the door. She turned back to say, "Be careful."

Chapter Twenty-Three

October 6, 1988

"Tomas?"

"Anna, what are you doing here?" Tomas jumped up from his desk and came around to grab her hands. A dark frown marred his features, and Anna responded defensively.

"I was going crazy," she said. "It's been almost a week. Besides, I waited till your secretary left for lunch." Her fingers tightened over his. "Have you heard anything?"

Tomas shook his head. "Not a word."

Anna dropped into a nearby chair and let out a

groan. "I hate this. What about the plebiscite? I can't make head or tails of what they're saying on TV."

"Rumor has it the 'no' vote won." She jerked upright. Tomas crouched beside her and kept his voice low. "Rumor also has it that Pinochet wants to overturn the vote."

Anna felt the blood drain from her face. "But he can't."

Tomas shrugged. "Who's to stop him?"

Anna slumped back against the cheap vinyl of the chair. "Even if the film and the story get through, it may already be too late."

"I don't know," said Tomas. "Let's not go looking for problems." He frowned at her again and stood up. "You know you shouldn't have come here."

"I brought a few bits of my book." She held up a canvas briefcase. "There's been nothing on the news or in the papers about Maria and Padre David. Have they found them?"

"Yes." Tomas perched on the edge of his desk, eyebrows puckered. "I'm sorry about Maria trying to hurt you."

"Did you ever love her?" She knew she shouldn't ask, but she'd wondered.

"I thought I did," he said. When he realized she was waiting for more he sighed. "When I met you, you saw no one but Romo. After Luis was born, I knew I had to leave or go crazy. I met Maria on a beach and she reminded me of you. But she wasn't."

"I'm sorry, Tomas."

"The police have been to see me," he said, changing the subject. "So far they've said very little."

232

"Didn't they ask you any questions?"

"Not many." He stared into space over her head for a minute, then met her questioning look. "I think they already know a lot about what happened, but haven't necessarily connected it with me yet. Or they're waiting."

"For what?"

"For a mistake."

"Be careful, Tomas," Anna said. "I don't want to lose you, too."

Tomas gave her a tired smile. "Sure. They can't prove anything. There's no paper trail or evidence."

"Paper trail," she murmured. Her eyes widened. "Oh my God, Rico's package. They must have picked it up. What are we going to do?"

"Relax," he said. "Rico tossed it in the trash can before they picked him up. I came back and got it after my guy didn't show."

"What did you do with it?"

"Destroyed the entire package."

"What?" she cried.

"What did you want me to do? Keep the packages till someone came looking for them? Then they could come looking for you."

"Sorry." Anna thought about the risk he'd taken to come back and destroy Rico's package as well as his own. The risks he'd taken all along. For her. And for Romo. "What do we do now?" she said.

"Wait."

"But I want to *do* something-"

"Anna, whatever you do now would only put both of us in a great deal of danger." Tomas slid off the desk and paced around the crowded office. "I don't like this either, but I'd like to keep both of us alive, to say nothing of Pablo and Luis."

"And Romo."

"Of course. And Romo." Tomas stopped at the window, staring out its dingy panes with his back to her. Anna wondered what he was thinking. He turned to her again. With the light coming in behind him, Anna couldn't see the expression on his face.

"Assuming your package got through, it may take time to get it to the right people. A week isn't that long, even though it feels like it to us." Anna nodded. "Right now, the best thing for you to do is to go home, and I'll call you as soon as I hear anything. Will you do that?"

"All right." Anna stood up. "But you'll let me know right away?"

"I promise," Tomas agreed.

Without another word, Anna left the office.

Anna stood at the stove pouring a cup of tea. Lunch was impossible given the state of her stomach. Her nerves took another jolt when someone pounded on the back door. Her hand slipped and hot tea splashed all over the stove.

"Damn!" She set the kettle down and opened the door. Her heart lurched at the sight of Emilio's angry face. He must have heard about Maria.

"What the hell have you done?" he said. Emilio stormed past her into the kitchen, a newspaper crushed in his hand.

"What are you talking about?" said Anna. Difficult to play dumb, but essential. She closed the kitchen door, then went back over to the stove. With shaking hands, she laid a towel on the puddle. "Do you want a cup of tea?"

"No," he said and thrust the newspaper under her nose. "Take a look at this."

Anna took it from him. A glance at the masthead told her it was a Miami paper. She scanned the front page. It took three tries before she found it. The photographs. She moaned. Romo was almost unrecognizable. His hair and beard were long and straggly. It looked like he had a scar on his left cheek and he appeared gaunt. She smoothed the wrinkled picture with one finger and turned to Emilio.

"Where did you get this?"

"Oh, don't just look at the picture, my dear," he said. The barely suppressed fury in his voice belied the polite words. "Be sure to read the article next to it."

Anna searched the columns around the photographs and found the article. She read it, aware that Emilio was watching her. Instead of being paralyzed by her fear, Anna found her mind was calm and clear. Emilio's attention could be used to her advantage. A look of shock on her face would be natural. If he figured out that she'd smuggled the article and photos out, she was lost. Anna forced herself to read the entire article, and gasped in the appropriate places. Meanwhile, a sense of exultation grew inside her. She had done it. Her package got through. When she finished, she looked at Emilio with the mingled anger and bewilderment she'd had to hide when she first found out he'd killed her parents.

235

"Is this true?" she said.

"Is it true?" His face contorted with rage. "You lied to me! You knew where that article was all the time, and just waited for the right time to get it out!"

"I what?" said Anna. "What are you talking about?"

"You had it all along," he accused. "You betrayed me."

He believes that, she thought. He sees himself as the hero, who saved me from soldiers and a fate like Gabriela's. In his mind, I should be grateful to him.

Emilio snatched the paper from her. "Where did you find the article? And how did you get those pictures? That information just might save my life, not to mention yours."

"I never saw those pictures before," she said, knowing that technically what she said was true. She'd only seen the undeveloped film that night.

"And the article?"

Anna sat down and took a deep breath before she spoke. "Emilio, this doesn't make sense. The article says you killed my parents." She stopped to brush away a lone tear that trickled down her cheek. "If it's true, and you *did* kill my parents, and if I've known about it since Romo's arrest, do you really think I could have touched you, or let you touch me?"

She could see she'd scored a point. He sat down across the table from her, his face blank. The only time she'd had to sleep with him since finding out about her parents was the night Luis had walked in on them. Emilio hadn't required anything other than her presence that night. She didn't know if she could have handled more. He sat and stared at her, his hands

236

folded, his back straight.

"I'll have some of that tea," he said.

She got up, mopped up the remains of the spill, and poured two fresh cups of tea. She placed one steaming cup in front of him, and took the other back to her seat. "Why are you so upset?" Anna said. "This couldn't hurt you now, could it?" She hoped that last part didn't sound too hopeful.

Emilio glared at her. "It doesn't matter when it happened, it's a bad time for bad publicity. The article says that I had the support of the coup leaders." He caught himself. "That is, if any of it were true. True or false is irrelevant. It couldn't have come at a worse time."

"*Did* you kill my parents?" she said.

Emilio sipped the scalding tea. "I don't know how Romo came by that information, but it isn't true," he said. "Your parents were my best friends. I could never have hurt them."

Anna wanted to throw her tea in his face, but controlled the impulse.

"How did the paper get a photograph of Romo in prison?" His voice was sharp.

Anna went on the attack. "How would I know? You never told me where he was, or even if he was still alive. How could I have found him?"

Emilio was silent. Anna stole a look at him. He was staring into his cup, at a loss for the first time in all the years she'd known him. It occurred to her that he might be scared.

The doorbell rang. They both jumped. Anna went to answer it, with Emilio on her heels.

She opened the front door to another shock. It was Juanita. In a soldier's uniform. With four soldiers behind her. A rush of fear shot through Anna. Had they come to get her? Juanita looked over Anna's shoulder and Anna remembered Emilio, silent behind her.

"May we come in?" asked Juanita. Anna nodded and backed into the living room. Juanita motioned to the soldiers to wait in the hall and followed Anna.

Anna wondered why Emilio was so quiet. Soldier or not, Juanita worked for him, and he was an important man.

"What is it?" said Emilio. His voice was calm and dispassionate, and he stood close to Anna.

"I think you know," said Juanita. "The only question is Anna."

"What about Anna?" Emilio sounded bored and amused, but Anna heard the edge in his voice. Juanita must have heard it too, because she smiled grimly. She took a newspaper clipping out of her breast pocket and unfolded it. Anna could see it was the Miami clipping with Romo's article and picture.

"What does she know about this?" said Juanita.

Emilio shrugged his shoulders.

Anna's throat tightened. What if she hadn't convinced Emilio? Even if he believed her, he might turn her in to save himself. She could see the soldiers handling her as they had handled Gabriela. She could hear the screams of her sons when they came home, either to find her battered body or to find a similar fate for themselves. She swallowed hard.

Juanita never looked at Anna. She watched

Emilio. Anna was puzzled by her expression. It wasn't bloodthirsty or triumphant, or even malicious. It was as if she were waiting for something. Emilio remained silent.

"I'll ask you once more," said Juanita. "What does Anna know about the article and photo?"

Emilio glanced down at Anna. "She knows nothing," he said.

Anna's knees felt weak.

"Nothing?" said Juanita. She arched her eyebrows. Emilio's eyes met Anna's, and he nodded.

"Nothing," he said. His voice was firm and clear.

Anna was baffled. She had seen from his look that he felt certain she was responsible. She hadn't fooled him. Yet he was protecting her instead of turning her in and saving himself. Why?

"Are you sure?" said Juanita. She smiled at Emilio. "If you like, I'll let you watch while they get the truth out of her." She gestured at the soldiers.

"I said she knows nothing," Emilio snapped, "And I meant it. Now let's go."

The soldiers handcuffed Emilio and hustled him out of the house.

Then, for the first time, Juanita turned to meet Anna's eyes. Her gaze was unreadable, and she was no longer smiling. "I suggest you be very careful," she said. She started to say more, then stopped and marched out.

Anna went to the door. Emilio's gray head was visible through the rear windshield, and she watched them drive out of sight.

As soon as they disappeared around the corner, Anna slammed the door shut and raced back into the kitchen. She picked up the paper and pored over the picture and article. She checked the masthead again. It was yesterday's paper. Had it been in time to save Romo's life?

She picked up the phone and called Tomas. His secretary tried to put her off, but she insisted on speaking to him.

"Anna, what is it?" He sounded annoyed.

"Emilio was just arrested."

"What?"

"He showed me a Miami newspaper. The pictures and the article were published yesterday."

"That's great," Tomas said. "But why was Emilio arrested?"

"I guess those arranged accidents were never supposed to surface. Now he's embarrassed the government, and with the plebiscite he claims it's bad timing."

"Right. Are you okay?"

"Yes," she said, her voice shaking. "I really am okay. Juanita tried to get Emilio to implicate me, but he said I didn't know anything. I guess he figured it was safer for him." She wasn't prepared yet to tell Tomas that Emilio had saved her at his own expense.

"Do the boys have soccer tonight?"

"No," said Anna. "Why?"

"I just think it would be safer if you could all stay home."

"But don't you want to see the paper?"

"I can't get away right now," he said.

"I have time to run over before the boys get home."

Tomas hesitated. "I'd rather you didn't. I can see it tomorrow."

"Don't be silly. I'll see you in half an hour." Anna hung up before he could object. She needed to get out, and Tomas was the only one she could talk to anymore.

A red Jeep pulled into the parking space right in front of Anna. She muttered under her breath and drove around another corner. A quick glance at her watch told her she'd have to be fast to get to Tomas' office, drop off the paper, and get home before the boys. Traffic had been heavier than she expected, and she heaved a sigh of relief when a convertible pulled out of a space in the next block.

Hurrying up the sidewalk toward Tomas' office, Anna clutched her handbag to her chest. Inside was the newspaper, the proof of her success. At least, it was a success in getting the goods through. Now if only Tomas could find out if she'd been successful in keeping Romo alive.

She rounded the corner and came to an abrupt stop. There was a crowd of people in front of the entrance to Tomas' building, along with the flashing lights of police cars. It didn't matter, she had to get in to see him. A discreet push here, wiggling through there and Anna was at the door.

The elevator took forever to get to the fifth floor. Anna opened the door to Tomas' outer office and gaped. His secretary sat at her desk, sobbing, while a policeman stood over her. They both looked up when the door opened. Anna stepped inside.

"Is there something wrong?" she said. "Where is Tomas?"

The secretary burst into another round of sobbing, and the policeman crossed over to Anna.

"Were you a friend or business associate of Señor Ugalde?" he said.

"Were? What do you mean 'were'? Where is Tomas?"

"I'm very sorry," said the policeman in a polite, smooth voice. "Señor Ugalde has met with an accident. We believe he committed suicide."

Anna reeled. It wasn't possible. Tomas couldn't be dead. He would never commit suicide. He hadn't sounded depressed in the least when she'd spoken to him less than an hour ago.

Suddenly it clicked in her mind. The flashing lights. The police. They'd caught up with Tomas about Maria's death. He hadn't committed suicide, they'd killed him somehow and made it look like an accident.

Something in her face must have given away her thoughts, because the policeman's eyes narrowed. He went to Tomas' office door and spoke quietly to someone inside. While his back was turned, Anna slipped back outside the door and ran to the elevator. Her heart pounded while she waited for it to come. The doors opened and she was inside the elevator when Tomas' outer door opened again.

"Señora, wait!" Two policemen ran toward her as the elevator doors slid shut. She leaned against the wall and closed her eyes. They flew open again. Those policemen weren't going to meekly give up on following

242

her. They were probably running down the steps chasing the elevator while she was trapped inside.

The floor numbers passed by too slowly for Anna. She stood poised at the door, waiting for the first crack to open up. As soon as it did, she squeezed through and ran out the front entrance of the building. Pushing and shoving her way through the crowd, Anna reached the corner and looked back. The two policemen were just running out of the building. She ducked around the corner before they spotted her, and walked quickly in the direction of her car.

Chapter Twenty-Four

"Mama, can we turn on the TV?" Pablo said. He cocked his head, fork halfway to his mouth.

"Don't you like Luis and me?" she teased him.

"Nobody wants to talk tonight," he said. Anna exchanged glances with Luis. Pablo was right. Luis was still angry, although part of that anger was directed at Emilio. She hadn't told him about the arrest yet, but it wouldn't make that much difference. It would take a long time for him to forgive her.

"All right, turn it on," she said.

"Thanks," Pablo said. He jumped up and hit the power switch, quickly absorbed in the cartoons on the screen. The little portable black and white TV had originally been bought for Anna to watch while cooking, but Pablo was the only one who used it on a regular basis.

Anna cleared the table and brought over the chocolate tortas she'd made for dessert. Pablo reached out for one without taking his eyes from the screen.

Someone rapped on the glass of the back door. Anna shook her head at Luis, who was halfway out of his chair, and went over to the door. Pablo was oblivious, glued to the TV and his torta. Anna peeked through the window curtain and gasped. She threw the door open. It was Romo. Emaciated. Worse than in the photographs. But it was Romo.

"Papa!" Luis jumped up from the table and ran to embrace his father.

Anna wanted to go to Romo, but her feet wouldn't move. It was like one of those dreams where people are moving in slow motion. The picture in the paper hadn't prepared her for the transparency of Romo's skin and the bruises that discolored his face and arms.

Romo reached out a hand to her and she grasped it with both of hers. She flinched at the touch of his cold hand, rough as sandpaper, and remembered how warm and powerful his hands had been.

"Come inside," Anna managed. She closed the door. She knew she should kiss him and hug him, but Luis held him tight in a fierce grip. She poked Pablo to get his attention, and turned off the television. Pablo looked up.

"Papa," he said, as calm as if he'd seen his father yesterday. "What did you bring me?"

"Pablo!" Anna cringed at her son's callous self-interest. Romo smiled, released Luis, and held out his hand to Pablo. Pablo ran to Romo and threw himself into his father's arms. Romo staggered slightly, but his face glowed as he looked down at the two boys.

"What happened Papa, why are you so dirty?" Pablo said. Romo smiled at him again. "I guess I need a bath," he croaked.

Anna could have cried at the pathetic shadow of a voice he had left. What had they done to damage his voice like that? "Let your father sit down, boys."

Luis pulled out a chair and Pablo tugged at his father's hand, dragging him over to the table. Anna brought over some leftovers from dinner and sat down across from Romo. Pablo stood, leaning against his father, while Luis sat next to him in a chair pulled as close as possible. Romo ate very little, but drank several cups of coffee. There wasn't much they could say in front of Pablo, for which she was grateful.

Anna felt peculiar. Romo was home. She should be happy, and she was. But he wasn't the same Romo who had left. The old Romo would have talked non-stop through his dinner, with a ready laugh and piercing intelligence. This Romo was silent and grim, except when he smiled at his sons. She had gone through so much for this man, and now he felt like a stranger. A stranger who had asked for a divorce a lifetime ago.

Romo pushed his plate to one side. "What's happened while I was gone?" Luis glanced at his mother, then looked away. Anna could tell by his puzzled frown that Romo had seen the exchange. Pablo chattered to his father, and Romo's frown dissolved into a grin at the irrepressible enthusiasm of his

246

younger son.

"Pablo, that's enough," Anna said. "You don't want to tire your father out the minute he gets back."

"It's all right, I don't mind." Romo turned to Luis. "But how are you? You haven't said much."

Before Luis could respond, there was another knock on the back door. Anna and Luis started.

"It's all right," Romo said. "I know who it is. Would you get it, Luis?"

Luis opened the door and stepped back to let Juanita enter, still wearing the uniform she'd had on earlier in the day. Anna jumped to her feet.

Pablo ran over to Juanita and grabbed her hand. "Our Papa's home. He's been away but he got back tonight."

"Yes, I know," Juanita said.

"Do you know each other?" Romo said.

"Yes," Juanita said. "I didn't have a chance to tell you before."

"What's going on?" demanded Anna.

"It's okay," Romo said. Anna folded her arms and waited.

Juanita put a hand on the boys' shoulders. "Can you two do something for me?" she said.

"Sure," Pablo said. Luis didn't respond.

"Go upstairs, and start a game on the computer. I'll be up in a few minutes."

Anna stepped forward to protest. Romo reached up a restraining hand and Pablo dashed off. Luis hesitated and looked at his parents. At his father's nod, he left the kitchen with a backward glance.

"What's going on?" Anna repeated. "Why are you here? Did you come back for me this time?"

"What are you talking about?" Romo said, looking from one to the other.

"I didn't come back for you," Juanita said. "You may find this hard to believe, Anna, but I'm your friend."

"You're no friend of ours," Anna said, gesturing toward the uniform. "You're in the army."

"My work in the army is a cover, and that's all you need to know about it. I arrested Emilio and brought your husband home."

"Why?"

"Could we sit down?" Juanita said. Anna took a seat beside Romo. Juanita sat down across from her. "I work with Tomas and Padre David, just like you." Her eyes clouded over. "I'm sorry about Padre David."

"You work with Tomas?" Romo said, turning to Anna.

"Yes," Anna said. Should she tell them about Tomas' death? It was hard to think clearly. "How do you know about Tomas and Padre David?" she said to Juanita. "Are you part of the underground?"

"You could say that. One of the reasons I came here to sit with your children was to keep an eye on them."

"You were taking care of the boys?" Romo said.

Juanita glanced at Anna, then smiled at Romo. "Anna can get into all the details later."

Anna's throat constricted. Juanita wasn't going to tell Romo about Emilio. Eventually he'd have to know, but not yet. Not until she could find a way to explain.

"How did you know about Padre David?" she said.

"Tomas called me," said Juanita. "I wish I'd known Maria was that far gone. Maybe I could have..." Her voice trailed off and she shook her head.

"Was Tomas involved in my release too?" Romo asked. Juanita nodded. "Then I ought to call and let him know I'm home." He pushed his chair back.

Anna laid a hand on his arm. "Wait a minute." Anna moved her hand to his shoulder and met his questioning gaze. "I went to see Tomas today. Right after you arrested Emilio," she said to Juanita. "When I got to his office police and soldiers were there. They said Tomas had committed suicide."

Juanita swore softly. Romo slumped forward onto the table, his head buried in his hands.

"It wasn't true," Anna said. "I'd talked with him this morning, and he wasn't depressed or upset. They killed him."

"Poor Tomas," Juanita murmured. "And just when you'd succeeded." She got up from the table. "I'll go up and join Pablo and Luis, or they'll be down to find me." She left. There was a long silence.

Anna stroked Romo's curly, black hair, now streaked with gray. So much to say. So much to hear. The months of prison had left their mark on Romo. Not only the gray in his hair and his gaunt frame, but also the lines carved into his face, the wariness in his eyes. One of Padre David's contacts had told her that torture destroys a person's faith in humanity. It becomes impossible to trust anyone completely after being tortured. Looking at Romo, she could believe it.

She stretched her arm around his shoulders. He sat up and caught her in a fierce embrace. She held him tight, feeling his bones jutting against her body.

"At least he died quickly," he muttered. She tried to pull back to see his face, but he resisted. "Emilio came to see me in prison." Anna stiffened. "He kept asking me about the article. Juanita said it was published in a Miami paper."

"Yesterday's paper," Anna said, her chin jammed against Romo's collarbone. She shifted her head to rest her cheek against his shoulder.

"The last time he came to see me," Romo said, his voice low and unsure. "He told me you were his mistress." She felt the uneven rise and fall of his chest against hers.

"Was it true?" he said.

"Yes." She waited for the explosion. None came. Instead, he lifted her hand to his face and kissed it. "I'm sorry," he whispered. "I'm sorry, querida."

A sob burst from her throat. The tears came for the first time since Emilio forced his way into her bed. One sob followed another, the release almost unbearable.

Anna heard footsteps, but she couldn't stop crying. A gentle hand patted her back. She lifted her tearstained face. It was Luis.

"It's all right, Mama," he said. "Papa's home now." Before she could answer, Pablo rocketed into the room.

"Why are you crying?" he said.

"We're happy to see each other," Romo told

him. Juanita followed Pablo into the kitchen. "We needed some ice cream," Pablo said. Luis gave his mother one last, shy pat, then helped Pablo get the bowls, spoons and ice cream.

Anna wiped the tears from her face with the back of her hand. Her thumb traced the path of Romo's tears.

"Would you mind if I put on the news?" Juanita said. "I want to know if there's any word on the plebiscite."

"Sure," Anna said. She got up and switched on the little television. For a few minutes it was chaos, with Pablo and Luis squabbling over the ice cream, the television blaring, and Romo trying to talk to Juanita. But when Pinochet's face flashed on the screen, even the boys fell silent. The newscaster's strident voice filled the room.

"*Earlier this evening the final results of the plebiscite were tallied, with 55% voting 'no'. The President announced that democratic elections would be held one year from this December...*"

The rest of his words were drowned out by the cheers ringing through the kitchen. Anna hugged Romo, the boys, and even Juanita.

"He didn't overturn the results," Juanita said. "I never thought he'd accept it if he lost."

Anna turned off the television.

Juanita broke the silence. "I should go now. I'll have work to do." With a pat on Anna's shoulder, she slipped out the back door.

Anna watched, while Romo pulled his sons into a tight embrace. He looked at her over their heads, and reached one hand out to her. She took his hand and

251

carried it to her cheek. This time it was warm.

33843804R00144

Made in the USA
San Bernardino, CA
12 May 2016